A Forgery in Marseille

BOOK THREE IN A SERIES

JANICE NAGOURNEY

CASTLE BRIDGE MEDIA
DENVER, COLORADO, USA

CASTLE BRIDGE MEDIA
Denver, Colorado

Cover photo by Elisa Schmidt/Unsplash. This photo has been modified.

FRENCH DECEPTION: A FORGERY IN MARSEILLE

ISBN: 979-8-9895934-9-1

To Margault

Prologue

Paris, 1972

IF SHE HADN'T RENTED THE apartment on Rue des Trois Frères perhaps things might have turned out differently, although fate has a way of catching up with you no matter where you go.

It was her first apartment. Three small rooms—their once-garish wallpaper had faded, but the walls still emitted a low scream of *I'm ugly.* The bathroom was so cramped that her knees rubbed up against the door when it was closed. And the kitchen wasn't much better: a sink, an ancient gas stove, and a tiny refrigerator. But as with so many 'firsts,' she remembered it fondly.

A grocery shop up the street sold produce and cheap wine in plastic bottles. Many years later, it would be immortalized in the movie *Amélie Poulain.* Tourists would trek up Rue des Trois Frères to say that they'd been there, done that—but that would be far into the future. For now, there was a slightly run-down, *après guerre* feel to the neighborhood. Gaston *le charbonnier* carried bags of coal up to the building's apartments, his face and hands black with soot. She had seen him walking down the street one evening, scrubbed so clean that for a moment she didn't recognize him.

A telephone was a luxury item. De Gaulle had said that one communicated best by writing letters, or so she had heard, and few people had telephones. She had put her name on the waiting list, but she knew that she'd be out of that apartment before the phone lines arrived. For the time being, she'd go to the nearby post office, or the big café on Rue des Abbesses, buy a token and make her call.

Her father had insisted that she go to law school. The law was not of great interest to her, but enrolling in law school was the only way to escape from her sheltered upbringing in the provinces. She made sure that she passed all her courses; if she didn't, her father would put an end to her Parisian adventure. But to relieve the tedium of her studies, she was out in the neighborhood bars most evenings.

That was how she met a tall, olive-skinned boy with curly black hair and an engaging smile. He told her he was from the south, something she had realized just listening to him talk. No one seemed to know a lot about him, but that wasn't too unusual—people floated in and out of her group. He asked if she could put him up, just for a few nights. He started by sleeping on the sofa but moved quickly into the bedroom.

There had been unrest in the country a century earlier. 1871 had not been the best of years in France: the defeat in the Franco-Prussian War and, above all, the suppression of the bloody uprising known as the Paris Commune. In a decision of political and psychological import, the French government voted to construct a minor basilica to commemorate these two events. The result was Sacré Coeur, straddling the Montmartre hill, at the highest point in the city.

With her current flat mate ("call me Sasha from the south," he laughed), they would walk up the hill to sit on the steps in front of the basilica. It reminded her of an elaborately decorated wedding cake, whereas Sasha railed against the building. Someone ought to blow it up, he told her; it's an insult to the memory of the Communards. Maybe so, she said, but you must admit that the view of Paris from up here is spectacular.

One afternoon she returned home to find that he had left: his tattered backpack and his few belongings were gone. Had she fallen in love with him? At the time, she wasn't sure about that, but regardless, he should have told her that he was leaving. Perhaps that feeling was a part of her bourgeois upbringing that she had yet to overcome. She rolled a joint, put Sticky Fingers into the cassette player. And later that evening, she went out to a bar down the street, Chez Denise.

The usual crowd was there—out-of-work actors, an interior designer, a couple of artists, an accountant, and an American student. He had thick, wavy brown hair that covered the tops of his ears and his neck. He wore little round granny glasses, his gray eyes blinking rapidly as he tried to keep track of the multiple conversations going on around him. If following the patchwork of phrases got to be too much, he'd release the tension by cracking his knuckles.

A titter of laughter the first time she met him: "You can practice your English with Ralph," her friends had said. She thought all Americans had perfect teeth, unlike the French. But Ralph was snaggle-toothed, sometimes covering his mouth when he smiled. He didn't smile that often, and she wondered if that was why.

He had told her he was from the United States, but he spoke with an English accent, just like her *lycée* teacher. Later that evening, as he continued to drink, he sounded more like an American. And smiled more freely. At two a.m., when Chez Denise closed, he asked if he could walk her home. She didn't mind, feeling the effects of the pot and all the wine she had had to drink. He helped her up the stairs. Leaning against his soft, round belly felt comforting. "Would you like to come in," she asked. He smiled—he hadn't thought it would be this easy. Afterward, he had to admit that the sex hadn't been great: too much wine, not enough passion.

But if the sex was forgettable, the evening was nevertheless memorable. They were sound asleep when the shock waves of an explosion rattled the windows. Ralph didn't move, but the sound startled her awake. She opened a window, looked outside, saw other heads looking down at the mostly deserted street, the only sign of life two drunks staggering along the sidewalk. Then, the wail of sirens started to pierce the still night. The following morning, they learned that a group of anarchists had blown off the top of one of the cupolas of Sacré Coeur, "to avenge the blood spilled by the Communards." She was excited: it could have been a prank played by Sasha and some of his friends.

She learned only a little more about Ralph than she had about Sasha. He had finished his legal studies in America and was now enrolled at the Sorbonne's French language course for foreigners. Everything French intrigued him: the language, the food, the wine, and the museums. Ralph talked endlessly about France but said very little about his family or where he came from.

She found his English accent pretentious but guessed that it masked some insecurity he felt about himself. Ralph did tell her that he found French women fascinating. She refrained from telling him that he was cloying, as she liked to practice her English with him. Ralph returned to the United States at the end of his course, and he faded from her memory like a piece of paper rinsed clean by the rain.

Law school bored her, and after two years, she dropped out and trained as a translator. Her father was not pleased, but he was reassured that she could support herself. Her years in Paris were punctuated by a succession of lovers, but none could replace the spark of excitement she'd experienced with Sasha. When she tired of working in Paris, she returned to her home in the provinces. Her parents were now both deceased, and she had the place to herself. Occasionally a smile would cross her face as she recalled her early days in Paris and the olive-skinned boy with dark curly hair.

CHAPTER ONE

November 2010
New York City

WHEN HE THOUGHT ABOUT IT much later, Eugene Spector realized how he could trace so much of what happened back to the day he met with Tony Perryman, the father of the boy who had called himself Thomas Smith.

Perryman lived in a duplex apartment on the upper floors of an historic building on Park Avenue, with the obligatory views of Central Park and the Manhattan skyline from the floor-to-ceiling windows that wrapped around the cavernous rooms. Eugene had persuaded his boss at the FBI headquarters to authorize his visit to Perryman in the hopes of discovering the backstory behind the document that Perryman's son Thomas had presented to Jacques Mornnais.

Jacques Mornnais. Eugene had spent the past months trying to get inside Bruno Edremal's head to discover some hook, some fact, to use as leverage to get Jacques to agree to share the dirt that he had collected on the good and the great in France. But so far, Bruno hadn't been particularly helpful, despite Eugene's best efforts to get closer to him. And now, he wasn't even answering his phone. Was he still in Lyon? Eugene didn't know and not knowing bothered him.

And then, speaking about things that bothered him, there was Alex. At times, she could be very forthcoming, but at other times, she played her cards close to her chest—but she wasn't the only one. He'd always found it difficult to share his innermost thoughts; how many women had walked away humming 'you're too secretive?' It was giving him cause to worry: if he didn't start to confide in Alex, perhaps she'd do the same.

He pushed these thoughts to the back of his mind—burying still older thoughts that had taken up residence years ago—as he rode the elevator to Tony Perryman's apartment on the eighteenth floor.

CHAPTER TWO

Trubenne

IT WAS A YEAR SINCE Alex Thornhill had left Washington, D.C. She had been looking for an adventure, and she'd indeed found that when she went to work for Jacques Mornnais and rekindled her friendship with Marie-Agnès Duvalois. In another respect, Alex had achieved what she'd set out to do as well: reconnect with her family and go back to the ancestral home at Trubenne. She had cracked her uncle Richard's icy veneer. And in her cousin Charlotte she had found a new friend.

Then too, she had met Eugene, her partner in a sometimes-problematic relationship. At times, he could be such good company—warm, affectionate, considerate. Still, she felt that Eugene had erected an invisible wall, keeping prying eyes away from his more intimate thoughts. Today he was on his way to New York City to meet Tony Perryman; he'd told her that much, yet she knew she'd have to question him if she wanted to find out what had transpired. But it was more than that. What else was hidden behind those beautiful golden-brown eyes? She wished he felt the need to be more forthcoming. And, she wondered, was his quest to corner Jacques Mornnais a way to avoid talking about what lay behind the invisible wall?

Had her cousin Charlotte been at Trubenne, she imagined that they would have cooked a special meal to celebrate this first anniversary. But Charlotte was in Marseille, and Alex felt a tiny tremor of discomfort. She, too, would soon set her bags down in Marseille, not so much to plunge into the life of the city as to hide from Jacques Mornnais. But first she'd stop off in Lyon to visit Marie-Agnès and see her new restaurant. Eugene wouldn't return to Trubenne until after her departure, but he'd promised to join her for Thanksgiving, wherever she happened to be.

CHAPTER THREE

New York City

AS THE ELEVATOR SILENTLY SPED to the eighteenth floor, Eugene's thoughts turned to the man who had called himself Thomas Smith, found shot to death in the Square des Batignolles in Paris. Alex had managed to make a copy of the document that Smith had left for Jacques Mornnais. Smith's hypothesis: Jacques was robbing the very people he featured in his magazine *Artixia*. Smith's proof: none. But there had to be more to it than that. Thomas Smith was a pseudonym—his real name was Thomas Perryman, son of the trader Tony Perryman. Had Thomas confided in his father, were there threads linking Jacques to the thefts? Eugene was about to find out.

An elegant woman—preserved to the best of their abilities from the onslaught of age by a multi-disciplinary team of professionals specializing in the art of appearance—greeted him at the door. When he introduced himself, she nodded and led him down a long corridor; to one side he glimpsed a living room the size of a football field, but she left him no time to take a closer look. At the end of the corridor, they entered a small alcove where she knocked and pushed open a carved wooden door hung with brass hinges: "Tony, your guest has arrived." She stepped back and held the door open: "Please."

In between the floor-to-ceiling windows, bookshelves lined the walls of the room. Tony Perryman stood up to greet him, "Special Agent Spector, please, have a seat." The man was of medium height and build, with close-cropped gray hair. He had the permanent suntan of his class, his face set in a cold mask. Seated again behind his desk, his hands interlaced, his neck and head rigid: "How can I help?"

Tony Perryman had reluctantly made time to see Eugene; he couldn't just refuse to meet an FBI agent investigating his son's murder. "There's not much to tell, Special Agent Spector." He seemed to enjoy using Eugene's title . "Tom was a nice boy, but no drive, no ambition." It sounded to Eugene as if he were describing the son of a friend rather than his own child. "As you know, the police think it was a crime of opportunity—Paris is such a dangerous city."

"I see," Eugene said. "Still, it looks like your son thought there could have been some connection between the theft of your Mondrian painting and you being featured in *Artixia*. We were wondering if he had said anything about that to you."

Perryman laughed, a cold, mirthless sound. "Yes, he left a message on my phone that he'd found my Mondrian. Said he'd discovered a ring of art thieves, of all things. Of course, that was ridiculous. Tom had no desire to do big things or be successful. If he wanted to, I could have helped him make a business career. But he was happy to study art history. As I said, the image of Tom sleuthing around, trying to find a band of thieves, was just ridiculous.

"Nevertheless, I spoke to Jacques Mornnais, and he said he'd ask around, let me know if he heard anything of interest. With his connections, I'm sure he's as likely as anyone to know about this ring of art thieves. With all due respect to the FBI."

Indeed, thought Eugene. Tony Perryman stood up, signaling that the interview was at an end. As he did so, he reached for an envelope on the corner of his desk, "You may as well take this," he said, "It came for Tom about a week after he was murdered. I doubt there's anything of interest, but you never know." He walked around his desk and opened the door to the office. Eugene had been dismissed.

\#   \#   \#

Eugene was eager to return to his hotel room. He'd found Tony Perryman insufferable; did the man ever lift his gaze from his navel? Asking the question provided the answer.

He looked at the envelope and saw that it was postmarked in Paris. He ripped it open and pulled out a bundle of hand-written pages; on the top of the pile was the document Alex had managed to copy and sneak out of Jacques' office. Eugene guessed that Thomas had sent the file to himself, probably to show to his father, not that that would have interested Tony Perryman.

As he skimmed through the notes, Eugene could sense the tension in the block letters, the pen's point digging into the page. Starting with a series of coincidences—paintings featured in *Artixia* turned up stolen shortly after appearing in the magazine— the young man had turned the coincidences into suppositions and ended up accusing Jacques of theft. Although it was a compelling story, it was built on the weakest of foundations: mistaking dreams for reality.

Yet Eugene smiled. What was reality in the face of appearance? He'd make a last attempt to contact Bruno, try to see if any useful recollection surfaced in Bruno's mind. But, if he couldn't extract any compromising information from Bruno, then he'd leverage the appearance of impropriety, ignoring the reality of proving it. In France, the smear—even the threat of a smear—could be a potent weapon in the right hands. Jacques of all people would know that, and Eugene was prepared to give it a shot.

CHAPTER FOUR

Marseille

BRUNO LOOKED OUT THE WINDOW as the train emerged from the long tunnel between Aix-en-Provence and Marseille, and saw the blue sea sparkling in the sunlight, reflecting the cloudless Mediterranean sky. He remembered a cheap hotel on Rue Breteuil, surrounded by lawyers' offices, checked in there, and made a phone call. After lunch at the Café de la Banque, he walked over to Rue Saint-Jacques and rang the bell at the Law Offices of Sauveur Paoli.

Time had not been unkind to Sauveur: sun-tanned from sailing year-round, the grey strands in his dark hair giving him a distinguished look, his body still firm from daily workouts. If his face was weather-beaten, it only added to his charm. He came out of his office, hugged him, and kissed him on both cheeks: "Bruno, my old friend, how are you?"

Bruno told him he had worked for Jacques Mornnais until last January; after that, he had spent some time with his sister in Lyon. Nothing untrue, but not the whole truth either. He had decided to return to Marseille and was looking for work. Sauveur said he thought he might have something for a man of Bruno's talents.

"By the way, how is our friend Mr. Mornnais? I heard his wife was in a fatal car accident."

"Yeah, that was after I had left, so I can't say anything about it."

"A pity anyway. I guess you don't know, but he sold me a magnificent painting by Paul Signac just a few months ago. I mentioned it to one of the curators at the Musée Burlotti; it turns out that they're planning an exhibition of the Pointillists, and they might want to include my painting. They'll be coming to view it in the coming weeks."

Let's see how good Li and Wen were. I'd love to be there if Sauveur discovers that Jacques sold him a fake.

#   #   #

Bruno wanted to test his memory, to see how many recollections—whether welcome or not—had returned. He walked over to Boulevard Notre-Dame and climbed the stairway that led to the Notre-Dame de la Garde Basilica. Marseille's best-known tourist attraction, it stood on the highest hill, overlooking the sea. He remembered that he had liked to come up here when he had lived in Marseille, the site had reminded him of the Fourvière Basilica in Lyon. He sat on a stone bench built into the side of the church. It was late afternoon now, the sun low in the sky, a cold wind whipping the water below, like white chalk marks on a blue-gray slate.

It was time to move on. Bruno walked back through the village of Vauban that hung on the hillside. He passed a small white house, its blue shutters closed. A taxi blocked the narrow street; the driver was unloading a large red suitcase. Bruno paid no attention to the passenger—an older woman with white hair—as she dragged her luggage up to the front of the house. For a moment, she fiddled around with the key, then the door opened, and she went inside.

CHAPTER FIVE

Marseille

THE HOUSE WAS COLD. CHARLOTTE Vesla de Trubenne went from room to room, turning on the radiators to get rid of the damp air. Once it warmed up, she'd lower them—she wasn't used to an overheated house. Although dusk had fallen, she felt an urge to go for a walk, explore the neighborhood. It was windy, and there were not many people on the sidewalks. She cut her walk short, stopped at a supermarket, bought as many provisions as she could carry, and returned to her new home.

Too tired to cook, Charlotte heated a frozen meal in the oven, poured a glass of wine, and remembered the other time she had been to Marseille. She had received a note from an old boyfriend, someone not on her mind every day, but not forgotten either, asking her to meet him in Marseille the following week. What had become of him, Charlotte had wondered. The next week, she'd taken the long train journey from Paris to Marseille and daydreamed about seeing him again. She wanted to feel his body against hers, run her fingers through his dark curls.

She had checked into an inexpensive hotel near the Vieux Port. The next day she wandered around the narrow streets and alleyways of the Panier, a neighborhood with a kind of rough charm that overlooked the Vieux Port. She arrived at the Bar des 13 Coins a little after noontime. And waited. She ordered lunch, imagined that any minute he would walk through the door. The restaurant had started to empty out when she concluded that he was not coming. She walked back down the hill, around to the other side of the Vieux Port, down to the Catalans beach. She continued along the Corniche until she reached the Vallon des Auffes, a tiny harbor with gaily painted fishing boats and old houses with multi-colored facades. The wind blew away her disappointment, and she returned to the restaurant in the evening, thinking that perhaps he had been delayed. He never came, and the following day she took the train back to Paris. She felt let down, incomplete, but told herself that it was better to accept what was then to yearn for what wasn't.

#   #   #

The years working in Paris had been followed by the years at Trubenne. She'd been snug in the run-down family château, each day of her uneventful retirement very much like the other, and she'd started to ask herself *how much time was left?* The memory of the Vallon des Auffes had remained clear and fresh, and she started to imagine living near the sea. She wanted to experience life in its fullness, and what better place than Marseille, with its rich brew of cultures, perched on the edge of the Mediterranean? *I'm not unlike Alex,* she thought, *irresistibly drawn away from the comfort of sameness.* Time was like a passing comet; she would catch it by its tail and see where it took her.

CHAPTER SIX

Paris

THE PORTLY MAN SAT AT his usual table at La Belle Fermière. He had a full head of brown hair; it was thick, almost unruly. His eyes were small and gray, and there was something a bit too tentative, too non-committal, about them. As he was a lawyer, perhaps this was normal, after all.

Merv Peters was soon joined by a group of his peers. They all ordered the restaurant's famous fried eggs, the whites neither overcooked nor runny, the yolks perfect golden orbs. It was an ideal time to exchange gossip, discuss deals, network, see, and be seen. Breakfast finished, his companions left to continue their day, much like the previous one.

Merv ordered another cup of coffee and surveyed the wreckage: little bits of now-rubbery egg white stuck to the egg yolks' gooey remains; half-eaten pieces of bread; the sides of tall glasses pockmarked by the residue of freshly squeezed orange juice. He tried to remember how many times he had come here, how many people had joined him, calculate how many eggs they had consumed, and then he gave it up. *Same old, same old. If I stop coming, people will wonder if there isn't something wrong, but if I see one more fried egg, I'm going to start clucking like a chicken.*

On the banquette next to him, there was a copy of the magazine *Focus on Food*. He had bought it this morning on his way over to La Belle Fermière. While on vacation, the French will discuss plans for a future holiday, and, in the same vein, when in a restaurant, talk about other dining experiences, past and future. Merv was American, not French, but he had lived in France for so long that he could be forgiven for having adopted many of its customs. So, it was only natural for him to leaf through *Focus on Food*, looking for a gastronomic escape from his feeling of ennui.

The French elite, all of whom live in Paris, consider that city to be the center of the universe. This is evident in media reporting and weather forecasts, where news of the provinces is ancillary, at best. It was therefore normal that *Focus on Food* would concentrate on Parisian restaurants, with limited attention given to the rest of the country. Nevertheless, in this issue, a few pages were devoted to Lyon. And Merv's sluggish pulse picked up a bit when he read a glowing paragraph about a new restaurant called "Chez Blondie." *Authentic, yet original dishes, stunning décor, reasonably priced,* said the review. A short trip outside of Paris was just what he needed to clear away the collateral damage of the breakfast battlefield. He called and made a reservation for lunch the day after tomorrow.

#   #   #

Merv left Paris early in the morning, traffic was light, and despite the leaden sky, he felt buoyant, glad to shed the skin of Paris for even a few hours. He left his car in a parking garage near the restaurant.

His lunch lived up to *Focus on Food's* promise. Merv had been kind to himself: pan-fried artichoke and *foie gras*, followed by sweetbreads and truffles. For dessert, he chose an ice cream, citrus fruit, and pastry creation. With his body busy digesting the carbs and fats, Merv's brain slowed down. At first, he didn't notice Marie-Agnès Duvalois as she walked around the room, greeting diners. Then she was beside his table: they looked at each other, and it was hard to say who was more surprised.

"Mag?" he asked. The name "Marie-Agnès Duvalois" hadn't rung any bells; he had known her as simply "Mag."

"Yes, Merv," she smiled, "Welcome to my little *bouchon*."

"Great food, great service."

She thanked him, and looking for words to fill the ensuing silence, asked: "And how are you, these days?" It was all Merv needed to return to his current obsession, the questionable origin of the paintings in his secret garden.

"I'm thinking of returning to the US and selling my collection," he blurted out. "Are you still in touch with that friend of yours—what was his name—Weller, I think it was? Do you think he could be interested?"

"I really do not know, but you'll have to excuse me now, I need to visit my other guests. I'll call you if I talk to him," and she hurried away.

Merv left a short time later, without commenting on the large mural that adorned the rear wall of the restaurant. Merv was a smart man but saw neither the forest nor the trees, only the ground beneath his feet.

\#   \#   \#

An unwelcome thought: Can I never escape the world of Jacques Mornnais?

"What should I do," Marie-Agnès asked Tomas that evening. She hadn't said much to Tomas about how Jacques Mornnais had tried to have her killed. She hadn't gone into detail about Alex or Eugene or Richard. He knew of their existence, but he sensed that Marie-Agnès didn't care to talk about the past, and he didn't push her. She did mention that Merv had introduced her to Blondell Royston, the woman who had subsequently bequeathed the apartment on Place des Vosges to her. If only to explain how, with her sole income from translating, she came to have a small fortune.

Tomas didn't know who Mr. Weller was, and he didn't care. That was in the past, and what interested him was their restaurant in the here and now.

"It sounds like you don't want to get involved with this fellow Merv, do you?" he asked.

"No, not really."

"Then don't. You don't have to do anything. If he calls you, say you haven't heard from that guy Weller. Just drop it."

It was good advice. Unfortunately, she didn't take it but instead called Alex. Who left a message for Eugene.

CHAPTER SEVEN

New York City

EUGENE WAS ON HIS WAY to the airport when he read a cryptic message from Alex:

Merv Peters had dinner at Mag's restaurant and he said he'd like to talk to Carl Weller about selling his collection. Thought this could interest you!

The lawyer had slipped to the back of Eugene's mind, but he moved to center stage as the taxi pulled up to the curb: *this could be an opportunity to send an uncomfortable message to Jacques Mornnais.* Eugene called Merv: his friend Madame Duvalois had left a message that Merv would like to see him; he knew it was the last minute, but he'd be passing through Paris tomorrow, perhaps they could meet?

Paris

With ease, Eugene resumed his role as Carl Weller, a wealthy businessman interested in acquiring artwork. The last time they had met— it was Marie-Agnès Duvalois who'd made the arrangements—he had used Merv to obtain an introduction to Jacques Mornnais. And because of that meeting, Mornnais had been forced to refund the money Eugene's aunt had paid for a fake Nicolas Poussin painting. As it turned out, it had not been painless, blood had been spilled, but through no fault of Eugene's. At least that was how he looked at it.

#   #   #

Everything was the same. The same receptionist—"Can I offer you coffee or tea," she had asked—the same magazines and an untouched copy of *Le Figaro* for visitors to peruse. The office was the same as well. Files piled neatly on the long table, a large, clean ashtray next to them; the thick, dark green carpet; the hunting scenes; the polished wood. Merv, too, looked much the same, although Eugene noticed that his paunch had expanded since their last visit. *That's what comes from eating at Chez Blondie,* he thought.

The lawyer came forward to shake his hand, then returned to the large chair behind his desk. Eugene sat facing him, both feet on the ground, hands on his knees, leaning back: open, confident, and almost aggressive. He waited for Merv to begin.

"As I told Madame Duvalois, I'm thinking of selling my collection, moving back to the States. There are some magnificent pieces," he handed Carl Weller a folder—"Have a look at this information."

Weller skimmed through the document. It listed the name of the painting, its dimensions, and the previous owner.

"Hmmm, didn't you say that Monsieur Mornnais—the gentleman that you had introduced me to—didn't you say that he advised you in assembling your collection?"

Merv hesitated before he nodded, "Uh, yes, that's right,"

Carl Weller continued: "Your Monsieur Mornnais showed me a painting by Signac. It was a beautiful work of art, but all that he could tell me about the owner was that it was a trust in Singapore. When you consider the asking price—ten million US—that was a shaky foundation for such a grand castle, if you get my meaning. I didn't buy that painting, and I won't consider buying any of yours unless you can provide a chain of ownership back to the Stone Age."

As Carl Weller spoke, Merv managed a smile, "Of course, Mr. Weller. It may take me a little time to gather all the documentation, but I'll have the complete provenance for each of my paintings for you."

"Great." Weller stood up, they shook hands, and Merv showed him to the door. As soon as he returned to his desk, he called Jacques.

CHAPTER EIGHT

Château d'Hélène

USUALLY, HE WAS UNAFFECTED BY the weather—sunny or gray, rainy or clear skies—it was all the same to him. But today, he felt the heaviness of the thick clouds, smothering his energy with their dark shadow. He looked up from his desk, and for a moment, he expected to see Bruno—light-footed despite his heavy frame—walk into the room, but then he remembered that Bruno was gone. Not dead, unfortunately, but gone.

Jacques Mornnais didn't miss him, it was more like an old habit he had of looking up and expecting to see him there. He'd made some changes in his business, so it had not been necessary to replace Bruno. He didn't dredge up the past too often, but as the thought of Bruno lingered, it was joined by the image of Marie-Agnès Duvalois, the one Bruno had called the red-haired cow. He hadn't had much luck in getting rid of her either, not that it mattered now.

He called out to Mercie, the housekeeper who had replaced another Filipina, Ella.

"Yes, sir?" Mercie had a pleasant disposition, whereas he had always found Ella to be more reserved, perhaps even a bit surly. But she had been a better cook.

Well, you can't have it all. "Bring me a glass of mango juice, please."

Jacques heard a vehicle on the circular drive at the front of the château. He looked out the window—it was the truck from Top Pools, the company that was building his swimming pool.

The pool would be almost identical to the one he had seen at the home gallery of the antique dealer, Renaud Schneider. He would want to sell the château one day, and an indoor pool could only increase the value of his property. It would also allow him to map out and rehearse gaining access to the Schneider gallery.

He ran his hands through his thin, sandy-colored hair and pursed his lips in a simulacrum of a smile. The thoughts of Bruno had evaporated. He turned his attention to organizing the upcoming visit to the Schneider Gallery, in preparation for a lengthy article on the family and their collection of eighteenth-century furniture.

The piece would appear in his magazine, *Artixia*. The publication gave readers a glimpse into the lives of wealthy collectors, and being featured in *Artixia* stroked the egos of those featured in its glossy spreads. And, in the case of the Schneiders, it provided free publicity for their gallery.

The magazine didn't make money. Jacque's profits came about more indirectly: the visits to photograph and interview gave him ample opportunity to evaluate the alarm system and catalog the inventory for future transactions.

His phone rang, Merv Peters' caller ID flashed on the screen. Jacques' first impulse was to avoid talking with the pompous lawyer. Merv had steered some business his way, but Jacques still resented having to pay him for the services he had rendered. He had a second thought: Merv had facilitated his meeting Renaud Schneider. And perhaps the lawyer might continue to be useful in that respect, so Jacques would put up with him a bit longer.

"*Oui*," he said; it was not a greeting designed to put the caller at ease.

"Jacques, how are you? I haven't seen you since Nicolas Pagès's funeral."

"I've been busy." It was a neutral statement, but enough to send a chill of fear up Merv's spine.

"Well, actually, I have a bit of a problem. I've been thinking about selling my collection, moving back to the U.S., it's time for a change, you know what I mean? I took a closer look at the documents our friend Pagès provided when I bought the paintings, and the provenance is quite thin. I met his daughter, but she said that his records were missing. All these trusts and estates that sold the paintings, they must have gotten them from someone, right? So, I was hoping you could help since you worked with Nicolas...."

Merv's voice drifted off, as if waiting for Jacques to interrupt, to reassure him that he could indeed help.

"Why would you want to sell? The longer you hold on to the paintings, the more they'll increase in value. You're not short of funds, are you?"

"No, no, it's not at all like that, Jacques. I just want to move on, turn the page."

As he listened to Merv whining, Jacques had a momentary regret that Nicolas was no longer around to create the documentation the lawyer was looking for. But he'd been forced to remove Nicolas—and his files—once Eugene Spector had gotten his hands on the two identical forged Poussins. And how did that happen? It was all Nicolas' fault, and he'd paid the price for his ineptitude.

Jacques felt he could manufacture a chain of ownership for one of Merv's paintings, but certainly not all of them. He'd need to find another solution.

"I understand, Merv, yes, it's time for a change. Can you give me a week or so to check if I have anything that could help you?"

Jacques now regretted that he had answered the call, but since he had, it was time to request Merv's help, and he continued: "In fact, I've meant to call you," he paused before continuing, "I was hoping you could do me a small favor if you happen to see Renaud Schneider at one of your little breakfasts. I'd appreciate it if you could subtly remind him how being featured in *Artixia* can bring them exposure to the right audience. We're planning on going over to his gallery to do a shoot, and I wouldn't want him to get cold feet."

Relief washed over Merv, like a gentle, warm shower. He said that he'd be more than pleased to talk to Renaud Schneider, and repeated that he hoped Jacques could help with the provenance documents.

CHAPTER NINE

Marseille

A COLD, DRY WIND BLEW down from the north, hurtling plastic bags into the trees' bare branches, and whirling dead leaves across the sidewalks. The wind lifted laundry that had been left outside to dry on balconies and scattered it on the ground. Marseille was not a particularly clean city under the best of circumstances, and the wind wreaked havoc with whatever was not firmly anchored.

It had been gusting for two days. Charlotte awoke in the middle of the night as the howling wind rattled the shutters of her little house. She had a headache, and she wondered how much longer the windstorm would last. Was it the Mistral or the Tramontane? She didn't know, didn't really care, she just wished it would stop. In the meantime, she wasn't going to stay cooped up inside: she had not come here to stare at the four walls. She remembered the Catalans beach from her trip to Marseille many years ago—why not go there to admire the sea in its full fury?

The wind had swept the sky clear of clouds; the sun provided brilliant light but no heat. Under her anorak, she wore an electric blue cashmere turtleneck sweater that matched the color of her eyes, her hair pulled into a loose braided ponytail to keep it from blowing in the wind.

Charlotte walked down Rue Breteuil to the Vieux Port, her head hunched tortoise-like between her shoulders. As she turned onto Quai de Rive Neuve that led to the Catalans beach, two things happened: a strong gust of wind almost knocked her off her feet, and she suddenly felt famished. She had stopped in front of La Nautique, a restaurant floating on the water, and, eager to find food and shelter from the wind, she stepped inside, mounted a flight of stairs and was shown to the only available table.

A jumble of masts rocking gently in the wind surrounded the restaurant. Looking further out through the windows that wrapped around the large dining room, Charlotte glimpsed the Saint-Jean and Saint-Nicolas forts, and the Pharo Palace. And on the other side, the Canebière, a street that had seen much better days. Charlotte was delighted. Her headache disappeared as she savored a delicately seasoned purée of zucchini and goat cheese, followed by a seafood risotto.

She ate slowly, thinking about the events of the past year. Alex's arrival in France, Marie-Agnès going from rags to riches, Richard's newly found energy, the somewhat mysterious Eugene Spector, and the most unpleasant Jacques Mornnais. What would happen next, she wondered? No matter, she told herself, and ordered chocolate cake for dessert. Once, she felt someone's gaze resting upon her, but she saw no one staring at her, and returned to her reverie.

Across the room, a distinguished-looking man, tall, his thick dark hair streaked with gray, was discreetly studying her. He thought that the aquiline profile looked familiar, as did the way she held her head. Her white hair had been tousled by the wind; she had the rosy complexion of someone who spent time out of doors. He remembered eyes of an intense blue, but he was too far away to tell. As Charlotte finished her espresso, Sauveur Paoli rose and walked over to her table. Yes, her eyes were blue.

"Excuse me," he said gently, "but I think we know each other. You're Charlotte, aren't you?"

The voice grabbed her, wrapped itself around her chest, she strained to catch her breath. She knew it was Sasha before she saw his face, its olive skin weathered by years of sun and sea.

"Yes," she whispered, "I'm Charlotte, and I can't believe it, but you must be Sasha."

"May I sit down for a minute; I don't want to bother you."

"This is such a shock," she said. "I came to this city so long ago to meet you, you never showed up, and now I'm back for the first time, and here you are. This is almost too strange to be true."

"I know. I owe you an apology and an explanation. How long are you in Marseille? May I invite you to dinner?" He reached into his pocket and pulled out a card: "I'm no longer Sasha, haven't been for many years. My name is Sauveur Paoli."

Charlotte took the card and, without looking at it, put it into her purse. "Well…Sauveur, I've just arrived in Marseille; can I call you once I've settled in? I intend to spend the winter here."

He stood up and smiled. "Of course, Charlotte. Please allow me to tell you that you're as beautiful as ever."

Despite herself, she could feel the heat on her cheeks. "Not really, but it's nice of you to say so." He bent over, brushed his lips on the top of her head, "Goodbye, for now, I hope to see you soon," and walked out of the restaurant.

#   #   #

After lunch, Charlotte headed to the Catalans. Except for a lone figure walking a dog, the beach was empty. She sat on a bench, and stared at the sea, felt restless, got up, and continued to walk along the Corniche, stopping from time to time to watch the waves crashing against the rocks below. The wind and the spray brought tears to her eyes—at least that's what she told herself. After a while, she felt tired, turned around, and took the bus back to Vauban, wishing that she had never stopped to eat lunch at La Nautique.

CHAPTER TEN

Paris, Babs Tomason's apartment

MERV WALKED UP AVENUE FOCH from his apartment on Rue Lesueur. He turned onto Rue Lalo, where he entered an undistinguished looking building and rode the elevator to the sixth-floor penthouse. The paint could have used some refreshing, the carpet was frayed in spots, but still, it was a pleasant enough apartment. Barbara Tomason had inherited a collection of masterpiece paintings and eighteenth-century furniture, and that made up for the apartment's creeping shabbiness. She rented the apartment to Jacques Mornnais when he wanted to have a discreet meeting. With the revenue, she'd treated herself to a few visits to the plastic surgeon for a lift here, a tuck there. It was enough money to do some personal renovation, but not enough to redo her flat.

Eager to show off her new face and figure, Babs invited Merv and a few close friends to dinner. She hoped that it wasn't too obvious, and that her friends would just think that she was looking particularly well-rested and toned. Of course, everyone immediately noticed that she'd gone under the knife, but since she didn't say anything about it, neither did they.

There was a retired banker and his wife, a woman who imported clothing from the Far East and another couple. The woman was a writer, and her husband was, well, her husband. A favorite topic was the President, Bill Palmac, and his new wife, Alicia-Marie Petti; the group wondered how long their marriage would last. They moved on to the strikes last month: irritating, but part of life in France.

"Of course," said the writer's husband, "But the strike at the oil depots almost got out of hand. Energy is of strategic importance, you know."

The banker smiled, yes, but just as important as oil was the uranium that powered France's nuclear reactors. "Have you heard about the unrest in Brezikstan?"

"Where?" asked the clothing importer.

"It's that little country in Central Asia that supplies a large part of our uranium. Now, I would say that is of strategic importance, wouldn't you agree?"

At the mention of Brezikstan, Merv felt a pain in his stomach. At breakfast one morning, he had heard Jacques talking about how close he was to that country's government. He didn't care about that shitty little dictatorship, but the name reminded him of Jacques and all his problems.

After dinner, the maid served coffee and sweets in the living room. The clothing importer was admiring a small painting by Turner. "There's an art consultant, Jacques Mornnais, that keeps pushing me to sell, but I wouldn't part with it for all the money in the world, which he's certainly not offering, by the way." They all laughed, except Merv.

When an appropriate amount of time had elapsed, he stood up and excused himself: he had a long day ahead of him tomorrow. As Merv walked home, he thought that he had not explicitly asked Jacques if he could sell his paintings. If Jacques was trying to get his hands on Babs's Turner, then undoubtedly many of the works in his own collection should find buyers. Merv made his judgment on the evidence available to him, but the evidence was incomplete.

CHAPTER ELEVEN

Marseille

CHARLOTTE SAT AT THE KITCHEN table, sipping her coffee. Realizing now how hurt she'd been when Sasha had failed to show up so many years ago: something that she'd not been able to admit to herself at the time. And yesterday he'd walked into her life once again. Her first reaction had been to throw his card in the rubbish bin, but now she pulled it out from under eggshells and a lump of coffee grounds. How had he gone from being Sasha to a lawyer named Sauveur Paoli? Curiosity overcame disappointment, and she called him.

#   #   #

The Vallon des Auffes, a picture post-card pretty fishing village, seemed unchanged since she'd walked there almost four decades ago. Charlotte could not have imagined that one day she would be dining there with Sasha, or that his name was Sauveur Paoli.

Brightly colored fishing boats were anchored in the little port. Overhead, the highway between the Catalans and Malmousque ran across the iconic bridge with its three arches, high above the vast black sea. Beneath the bridge, a rocky formation jutted into the water. There was a row of fisherman's huts, and behind them, a restaurant was perched atop the rock, glowing in the dark November night. From their table, they could see the lights of the city on one side, and the illuminated bridge and Vallon des Auffes on the other.

At first, Sauveur did most of the talking. Charlotte listened, tried to smile, toyed with her glass of champagne. She had put on make-up, paid attention to her hair, chose a well-fitting Georges Rech black pants suit with a white silk blouse. Yet, she felt unattractive and lost, sitting across from a man who was a stranger.

"The night I left, we blew off the top of the cupola. A youthful prank, you might say. I wanted to tell you about it, but it seemed better if you didn't know anything."

"Yes," she smiled, "Better for me and better for you."

"Mostly you, Charlotte. You didn't know any of the others, except maybe the American."

"The American?"

"Yeah, there was a guy, I think his name was Ralph, who was supposed to be with us, but then he chickened out in the end. I never saw him again."

"But then, what happened when you sent me the message to meet you in Marseille?"

"Oh, that. I was still in my radical politics phase; I thought that revolutionary actions were needed to bring about change. I had been involved in some other things, and we suspected the police might want to talk to me, so I had to lie low for a while. I was really sorry that I couldn't meet you."

"But not sorry enough to let me know?"

"Believe me, Charlotte, at the time I couldn't."

"Well, anyway, that's all in the past. I see that you're no longer calling yourself Sasha…."

"No, Sasha is quite dead and buried. My real name is Sauveur Paoli, always has been. And I'm a lawyer, involved in real estate, that sort of thing. And you, Charlotte?

She talked about her life in Paris, about the move to Trubenne, about spending the winter in Marseille.

"I love this city, perhaps you would allow me to show you some special places?"

She felt too weary to protest that she was quite able to buy a guidebook and walk around by herself. "That would be very nice, but you must be very busy with your work."

"I'll tell you what, I love sailing year-round, especially when there's a good stiff wind. Perhaps I could take you for a look at the Calanques, they're really magnificent."

When Charlotte looked less than enthusiastic, he added, "Or, a friend of mine has a good-sized motorboat and perhaps you'd find that more comfortable. I'll call you when the weather is looking good: mild, sunny, and not too windy."

Charlotte felt that she'd been less than gracious, "That's sounds lovely, Sash, Sauveur."

He drove her home after dinner; they exchanged air kisses—in Marseille, it was left cheek first—and he promised to call soon. "It was so good to see you again, Charlotte."

"Yes, it was good to see you too."

At home, Charlotte removed her make-up and brushed her teeth. She thought of the American, Ralph, and wondered whether it had just been a coincidence that she had met him the night Sasha had disappeared. Then she replayed the dinner. Sauveur had retained his old charm, but—and there are always buts—she was curious how one went so smoothly from revolution to real estate. Richard would be back in Paris soon; why not ask him to mention Sauveur Paoli to his friend Michel de Clermont d'Auvergne, the next time they spoke.

CHAPTER TWELVE

Trubenne

AFTER HIS MEETING WITH MERV Peters, Eugene returned to the château. With Alex in Lyon and Charlotte in Marseille, Trubenne was already settling into the chilly calm of winter. He emptied his mind of thoughts of Jacques Mornnais and Alex as he painstakingly cleaned a *trumeau* over the fireplace in the living room. Leaves were intertwined with flowers, surrounded by scrollwork. It was an intricate design, and he enjoyed uncovering its hidden beauty. Richard came over to him; there was a room where they'd stored odds and ends over the years, and he wanted to get rid of as much of the junk as possible before he left for Paris. François Tran, who had helped with the renovation, would be coming over tomorrow. Could Eugene help them move the stuff out?

The next morning François Tran and his sons drove over in their van. They started to remove empty paint cans, boxes of broken tiles, skis and ski poles, moth-eaten clothing, bags of newspapers and magazines, chairs with broken backs or legs missing, a beat-up leather recliner, an old sofa: the litter of over half a century. One object happened to catch Eugene's eye, probably because it was so clean and shiny, so lacking in folds, wrinkles, and a covering of dust. It was a bright blue, yellow, and red Lidl shopping bag, leaning against the back of the sofa.

Eugene picked up the bag; there was something familiar about it, even if he'd never shopped in a Lidl supermarket. He thought back to the office he had rented at the Rond-Point on the Champs-Elysées; he and Alex had met there with Nicolas Pagès. Alex had brought a painting by Daubigny, 'Storm Over the Sea,' that they had asked the art dealer to examine.

He remembered that Alex had put the painting into a Lidl bag before slipping it back into a large shopping bag from Prada. How smart and nervy, he had thought, to walk around with such a valuable work of art in a cheap supermarket carrier bag. Later, she had given the painting to him. He had gotten a reward for Ella, the maid who had found it, and he'd returned the tableau to its rightful owner, a little church in Brittany.

Curious, he removed a parcel from the bag, pulled off the brown wrapping, carefully undid the bubble paper, and found himself holding 'Storm Over the Sea.'

"What the fuck," he muttered under his breath.

Richard walked past him, carrying a broken desk lamp: "Ah, that's Alex's painting, I wonder how it got mixed up with this junk. I'll put it in the salon with the others. We're saving hanging the artwork for the very end."

Eugene remembered the old priest to whom he had given the painting. So, there were two of them…which was a fake and which was real? He was disappointed that, once again, Alex had been less than forthcoming. Not that he had shared all his plans with her either. Hadn't he done her a favor by getting the reward for the maid? What was she up to? He just didn't get it. Of course, his actions at the time were not entirely disinterested, but Alex didn't know that. His disappointment hardened, and that evening he called his sister to say that he'd be coming to Alexandria for Thanksgiving after all. After that, he called Alex, asked about Marie-Agnès. Chez Blondie truly enchanting, she said. However, it still saddened her to think about Blondell Royston's death.

"Oh, by the way, I'm afraid I won't be able to join you right away, I need to spend Thanksgiving with my sister." He wasn't sure if he heard the disappointment in her voice, but since they were both adept at hiding their emotions, it didn't concern him very much.

CHAPTER THIRTEEN

Alexandria, Virginia

EUGENE COULDN'T GET ALEX AND the Daubigny painting out of his mind. Had he acted too rashly when he pulled out of spending Thanksgiving with her? Should he have pretended that he hadn't found the painting? *No,* said another voice in his head, *you did the right thing.*

While Eugene ruminated, Kate waved a duster over a credenza crammed with photos. There was a photo of her beloved aunt Madeleine—unsmiling, staring into the camera, the light sculpting her high cheekbones. Madeleine Connors, an aunt in name only. She had been a close friend of their mother, and, having no children of her own, doted on Eugene and his sister. She had married well, but her husband had died young, leaving her well off but with a wide gap in her life that she had tried to fill with the Spector children.

Watching Kate, Eugene couldn't decide if his sister reminded him of a sparrow or a hippopotamus. She had a way of waving her arms that made him think of a little bird fluttering its wings. But she also had a seriously generous derriere, and she walked in the deliberate way of large animals. Sparrow or hippo, he loved her just the same.

He knew that she'd been disappointed that the painting she had inherited from her aunt Madeleine was a fake. Still, Kate had taken comfort in the reimbursement that he'd gotten from the seller. How had he managed to do that, she'd asked. Did it really matter, he'd replied. The important thing was that the forger had been called out and made to pay. And how had that happened? Thanks to Alex and her friend Marie-Agnès Duvalois. The thought brought 'Storm Over the Sea' back to center stage; *maybe I ought to call Alex, just to see how she's doing?*

With a start, he realized that Kate was talking to him: would he *please* go down to the basement and sort through the boxes he had brought over when he moved out of his last apartment? He pushed the Daubigny aside and made his way down the stairs to the basement.

A lumpy sofa was pushed against one wall, the beige velour upholstery was rubbed thin, the flat cushions looked like limp marshmallows, and in one corner, his storage boxes were piled perilously. Perhaps Kate was worried that they'd all come tumbling down and that she'd have the job of cleaning up the mess, so it was just as well for him to get rid of his junk once and for all.

Eugene unpacked his paper shredder, placed it on an ancient white Formica table, and got to work. A while later, he had filled several gray garbage bags with a sea of chewed up paper. There were still four of his boxes left— records that he might still need—and Eugene pushed them back against the wall. Hopefully, Kate wouldn't mind if he left those with her a while longer. To make room, he needed to move a carton marked 'Madeleine.' As he lifted it up, the bottom opened, spilling the contents on the floor. Theater programs, restaurant menus, a bunch of old Gourmet magazines, blank postcards from art exhibitions, matchbooks, flyers from candidates in races long since over and forgotten, a calendar from a Chinese restaurant, brochures, and a plastic bag full of correspondence. If it were up to him, he'd throw it all out, but he'd leave that up to Kate, and he started to fill one of his empty storage boxes with the contents of Madeleine's carton.

All that remained was the plastic bag that he picked up off the floor. Perhaps it was his imagination, but Madeleine had always had an air of secrecy about her. They knew that she had family in Ukraine, but she never talked about them, or about her childhood. He reasoned that now that she was dead, he wouldn't be invading her privacy if he had a look at some of those letters. He emptied the bag on the old sofa and began to sort through the correspondence. Some of the letters were written in spidery handwriting, some in a firm hand, others were written on old-fashioned typewriters. Luckily, she was pre-digital, he thought, otherwise all this would have disappeared into the ether.

Kate appeared at the top of the stairs, "how's it going," she called out.

"Just fine, making progress, you'll be pleased, but I still have some stuff to go through."

"No problem, take your time."

He had packed up the shredder, and he put most of the letters from Madeleine's friends on the Formica table. He skimmed through some of them: a mixture of gossip, reflections on growing old, bits of news about children and grandchildren, illnesses, and death. He was glad he hadn't thrown them away. Kate would probably enjoy reading them, giving her a glimpse into Madeleine's life in the second half of the last century.

A rusty paper clip held two envelopes together; they were typed on airmail stationery as thin as a butterfly's wings and covered with colorful stamps. He carefully slipped open the first letter. It was short:

Dear Mado, This is just a quick note to let you know that I have found a solution to my problem. I'm not proud of what I've done, but I had no choice. Soon my debts will be paid, and I will be a free man again, above all, free from fear. I hope you destroyed my earlier letters as I had asked. I will write again soon and perhaps come to visit. Your loving brother, Viktor.

Eugene reread the letter. What was Viktor's problem; what was the solution he'd found; and what was he afraid of? Then he looked at his watch; soon, it would be time to go out to dinner. Eugene slipped the two letters into his jacket pocket. He'd have plenty of time to ponder the meaning of the letter he'd just read. As for the other letter, he would read it later, at his leisure. The rest of the correspondence went into the storage box; he turned out the lights and went upstairs. "All done," he called out to Kate.

CHAPTER FOURTEEN

Washington, DC

AS THEY HAD DONE PREVIOUSLY, Eugene and Kate passed on an invitation to join cousins once and twice removed for a marathon eat-fest, complete with an interrogation about what Eugene was up to these days. They preferred, as well, to avoid questions about their inheritance from Aunt Madeleine.

"You're looking well, did you do something to your hair," he asked. Kate had given up her topknot—"It made me look like my own grandmother"—and exchanged it for a hairstyle that made her head look like a pale-yellow artichoke. Her gray eyes glittered through an unruly white-blond fringe; "Do you really like it?" "Oh, absolutely."

In fact, he did like the change. On the other hand, he wasn't sure about Kate's apple green pants suit. He'd gotten accustomed to Alex's understated, 'black is my favorite color' style. But as he looked around the restaurant, he noticed enough color to fill an Impressionist palate: powder blue, lime green, cherry red, canary yellow….

Alex. Where was she spending Thanksgiving? Should he have joined her and asked about 'Storm Over the Sea?' He didn't think so, and he'd been right not to confide in her. Although perhaps he'd give her a call, just to see how she was doing…

"Thanks for clearing your stuff out of the basement. You know how I hate clutter."

"Excuse me?"

"I said thank you for clearing your stuff out of the basement."

"No problem. But I left a box of Madeleine's things—I thought that you might want to look through it. There was a plastic bag with letters from her friends. Seeing as how she's passed, I didn't see any harm in reading some of them. Really quite touching. Maybe you'd like to look through them one of these days."

"Funny that you mention Aunt Madeleine. I was thinking about her the other day," she said between mouthfuls of stuffing.

"And what were you thinking, Kate?"

"I was thinking that it was strange that she stopped talking about her brother back in Ukraine. Viktor, I think that was his name. She'd been so proud of him, and then, nothing—it must have been years and years ago, don't you remember?"

"Not really, but she must have had her reasons."

Eugene didn't mention the two letters that he'd shoved into his pocket, and he switched topics abruptly: "Since I got involved in helping you with the forgery, I've started to get interested in art. There's an Edvard Munch exhibition at the National Gallery ending in a couple of days— would you like to try to go tomorrow?"

#   #   #

The Munch show was a disappointment, not the prints themselves, but the crowd was so dense that it reminded Eugene of an airport right before Christmas. There were the irritating couples that stood shoulder to shoulder, one of the pair delivering an Art History 101 lecture. Then there were the people who insisted on bringing their small children—one couldn't blame the kids for being bored and unruly. And of course, chattering groups of teens. He had wanted to get Kate off the topic of Madeleine's brother, and the

Munch show was the first thought that popped into his head. Kate's reaction to the crowd had been to walk quickly through the exhibition rooms. She could be a bit of a snob when it came to consuming Culture; "I'm already quite familiar with his work, and I'm not prepared to play touch football. I'll see you later."

He walked over to 6th street, entered a nondescript building that housed a discreet FBI field office. Pascal Navarro, the Assistant Director, had his offices just below the top floor, as befitted his position. A visit to Pascal was not on Eugene's agenda; instead, he took the elevator down to the basement, where the archives were kept.

Mario Giuliano sat at a dark green metal desk in front of a steel gate. Behind the gate, thousands of files were stored, with access strictly limited to need to know. Years ago, Eugene had been Mario's platoon leader; he'd helped him through a rough patch when Mario had been a raw recruit.

As he saw Eugene approach, Mario stood up: "Ooh rah, sir."

"Ooh rah, how've you been?"

'Good sir, and you? I heard you've left the Bureau, gone to Europe."

"Well, that's mostly true, but I can't say much more. I need to check one or two things, mind if I have a look?"

If Eugene had asked Mario to walk through a minefield, he would have done it, no questions asked. So merely bending the rules didn't pose any ethical dilemma.

"Make yourself at home," he said as he unlocked the metal gate.

Eugene had read the second letter he'd found in Kate's basement. His curiosity was piqued—he wanted to learn more about Madeleine's brother Viktor—and he would spend the better part of the afternoon in the archives, seeing if he couldn't find the first premises of a backstory in the Bureau's files. It was a question of sifting through the files and, above all, connecting the dots. When Eugene put his mind to it, he was good at both tasks. "Semper fi," they said to each other when he left a few hours later. As he walked out of the building, he reflected that had he not bailed on Alex, he never would have found Viktor's letters and the first intimations of his own backstory.

CHAPTER FIFTEEN

Lyon

WHILE EUGENE WAS TENDING TO business in Washington and Charlotte was getting reacquainted with Sauveur, Alex spent Thanksgiving in Lyon, with Marie-Agnès and Tomas. Seeing how happy they were together, she felt a pang of jealousy: *why did Eugene have to be so difficult?*

When Alex visited the restaurant, her eyes were drawn to the mural, a wave of uneasiness engulfing her. "Did Li do this for you?" she whispered.

"Yes, and what do you think?"

"I see he's included all the usual suspects—he even included you. And Mag, I think it's fucking weird, don't you?"

"Not really. I find it kind of amusing, if you must know."

On the Sunday morning before she left for Marseille, Alex rose early. She took a leisurely walk through the market that stretched for a kilometer along Boulevard de la Croix Rousse. Fruits and vegetables of every color were arranged on tables on either side of the wide sidewalk, alongside stalls selling charcuterie, cheese, meat, roast fowl, paella, and couscous.

The damp, cold weather was a perfect excuse to step into a tearoom for a cup of thick, creamy, hot chocolate. For a moment, Alex thought that she saw Bruno walking into the shop, but as the man turned in her direction, she saw that she was mistaken. But the faces in the restaurant's mural stayed with her, reminding her of Jacques Mornnais, and she was suddenly anxious to leave Lyon and join Charlotte in Marseille.

#   #   #

Marseille

The day Alex arrived, the Mistral had stopped blowing and the sunlight soon warmed the cold air. They ate lunch on the patio, Charlotte laughing as she recounted running into the somewhat mysterious Sauveur. Alex described her stay in Lyon but omitted any mention of Eugene. For her there was nothing to laugh about.

After, while Charlotte ran out to shop for food, Alex wandered around the neighborhood; she found herself walking up Cours Pierre Puget, and arrived at the sculptor's eponymous garden. Passing the great man's statue that stood in front of a waterfall, she started up a winding path that led to the top of the hill. Alex had begun briskly but soon slowed down as the incline became steeper.

A man on a mountain bike sped around a bend— he probably drove his car with the same reckless abandon that he rode his bike. To avoid a collision, Alex jumped to one side of the road and landed on her back in some shrubs. The biker continued down the hill, this time narrowly avoiding a man who was jogging up the path.

"Asshole," cried the jogger, but the biker was gone. The man stopped running when he saw Alex struggling to extricate herself from the bushes.

"Here," he said, lifting her upright, "Let me help you."

"Thank you, what a jerk," she said, brushing leaves from her white parka, now stained by the muddy earth. He continued to hold her arm; it was only a few seconds, but time seemed to stand still.

"Don't I know you?" he said, "You're the blonde woman." He was sweating and pulled off his woolen cap to wipe his forehead. Where had she heard that voice before? Despite her warm coat, she felt a chill, realized that her knees were shaking: it was Bruno.

"Yes, we met in Lyon. Are you living in Marseille now?"

"Yeah, and you can tell your friend Eugene that I said hello." He pulled the cap back over his head, and resumed his run, jogging effortlessly up the hill.

Alex stood at the side of the path, deciding whether to continue her walk or turn back. *I'm not going to let any of this spoil my day.* As she reached the top of the hill, the sea came into view, a blue mirror gleaming in the afternoon sunlight. There was an open space with benches and a play area for children. It was deserted, except for Bruno, who was doing pushups and stretching his legs. He paid no attention to Alex, but when he had finished his exercises, Bruno turned, waved to her, and ran out of the playground and down the hill.

With Bruno gone, she felt more at ease and walked back to the spot where the sea came into view. In a short while, the sun would start to set, but before it did, she would sit on a bench conveniently placed in a patch of grass and admire the view. Eugene: Bruno had reminded her that she hadn't heard from him since he'd called to say he was spending Thanksgiving with his sister. Was he still there, she wondered? Why hadn't he called? Clouds rolled in, reflecting her darkening mood, and the color of the sea had changed to slate gray. It was time to head home. As if on cue, she felt her phone vibrating in her pocket and saw that Eugene was on the line.

CHAPTER SIXTEEN

IT WAS A SHORT CALL. Eugene was still in Washington—but he had plans to visit his friends in Lyon. Alex wanted to ask him if he'd be skiing again with them? But if he was, then why hadn't he asked her to join him?

"How are things at Trubenne?"

"Trubenne, oh, Richard closed the house up for the winter, why do you ask?"

"Oh, just curious."

It was a stilted conversation, punctuated by pauses that were too long. To fill in the space, she started by saying, "You'll never guess who," stopped herself from saying that she had just seen Bruno, and instead finished: "Charlotte ran into. An old flame. He's a lawyer here in Marseille."

"That sounds great," he said, no more interested than if she had given him a report on the weather.

She tried again: "Marseille is a beautiful city, I'm sure you'd love it."

"Yes, Alex, we'll have to arrange something in January."

"Okay, until then, have a happy holiday."

"You too, Alex, give my best to Charlotte and Richard."

Things had been so good between them at Trubenne, and now he sounded so distant. He'd probably met someone; it was the story of her life.

\#   \#   \#

If Alex was perplexed, Eugene was annoyed. With himself. *Why are you acting like such an asshole? Alex may have some explaining to do, but you need to give her the opportunity to do it.* He would call her once he'd arrived in Lyon and set things straight.

\#   \#   \#

Alex had reached the bottom of the hill and tried to lift her spirits by window-shopping on Rue Paradis. Temporary relief from her bad mood was provided by the purchase of an Armani ensemble: white silk blouse and grey tweed trousers.

On her way back to Vauban, Alex walked slowly up Rue Saint-Jacques, carrying her purchases. She glimpsed a man coming out of a building further up on the opposite side of the street; a first, she thought he looked like Bruno, and chided herself: *stop it! You've got to stop seeing him everywhere you go.* But as the figure stood by a motorcycle, putting on his helmet, there was no doubt that she was looking at Bruno. A moment later, he rode down Rue Saint-Jacques, the noise from the exhaust echoing off the buildings.

Alex walked up to the building. Three small bronze plaques were screwed onto the door: "Law Offices of Sauveur Paoli;" "Law Offices of Michel Paoli; "Law Offices of Monique Paoli." Wasn't Sauveur Paoli the name of Charlotte's friend? Had Bruno been to see him, or one of the other lawyers?

Suddenly, she felt glad that they were going to Richard's apartment for the holidays. Trubenne was still a work in progress, and she realized that the only place she could call home was the apartment in Neuilly, with its familiar furniture, its piles of magazines, and the collection of bibelots that she had found so kitsch but that now seemed strangely comforting.

CHAPTER SEVENTEEN

Marseille

THE THIN SNAKE OF VENGEANCE moved through his body, stirring up memories as he relived the past few months.

Bruno began with the moment Sandra had opened the door to her apartment in Lyon. "Bruno is that really you," his sister had said. He had made his way from the Part-Dieu train station to Place des Terreaux, and from there, he had walked up Montée de la Grande Côte. His thoughts continued to move back in time until Bruno saw himself crawling into the small cottage on the riverbank. His teeth chattered as he remembered the pain of being in the icy water.

His mind focused on the cottage, he remembered staying there, recuperating from those near-fatal minutes in the river. Once again, he was standing outside, staring at the château in the distance. His memory of that night stopped at the dinner table when the world went black.

Bruno couldn't stop reliving the events, again and again, thinking that if he rode the loop long enough, he'd figure out why he'd found himself in the river. Just as he was remembering Sandra opening her apartment door, his phone rang. He felt confused: was she at the door or on the phone?

"Bruno, are you OK? You sound strange."

"Yeah, I'm fine, I was just working on something, that's all. So, what's up?"

Precisely the question Sandra was waiting for. She launched into a tirade. There was no proof because there couldn't be any proof. But everyone at work suspected that she and Caroline Trabert had cooked up the embezzlement scheme together. She was miserable. Caroline had disappeared. And what was Bruno doing to find her and squeeze some of the stolen money out of her?

"I'm sorry," he said "But the last I heard she was in Thailand, and you can't expect me to go over there to look for her. If I hear anything, I'll let you know. Gotta run now."

Bruno's mood grew darker as the snake continued to slither. His mind started running away from him: perhaps Jacques was behind the incident at the river? As for the two men who had ambushed him at the Cour des Voraces, he was sure that Jacques had sent them to kill him. Bruno knew so much about Jacques' activities, and what he didn't know he could imagine. Now that Jacques had no further need for him, Bruno knew that his very existence was a threat. And he was only too familiar with Jacques' behavior when he felt threatened. Well, Jacques had tried to eliminate him once, maybe twice, but he wouldn't give him a third chance. Bruno thought again about the cottage along the riverbank and the nearby château. The thin snake of vengeance feasted on Jacques's wrongs, real or imagined. As it grew fatter, Bruno began to imagine his next steps.

CHAPTER EIGHTEEN

IN THE LAST DAYS OF November, Richard closed up Trubenne. He had never liked the winter in the Languedoc region. And despite the renovation, Richard felt the gloom of the château settle on him like a damp bathrobe, not unbearable, just uncomfortable. Now that everyone was gone, he preferred to return to his apartment in Neuilly. He'd visit his club, and see the shrinking circle of friends who, like him, had survived to experience old age. François Tran drove him to the train station; he and his sons would look after the place while Richard was gone, make it ready should Charlotte decide to return before spring.

The stay at Trubenne had done him good: the clean air, healthy eating, and increased physical activity had all energized him. It felt good, too, to be back in his apartment, to be spoiled by his housekeeper, Maria.

Richard thought of the Club des Deux Continents as a beacon in a stormy sea. Its steady beam indicating rocky shoals to be avoided, providing a guide to a safe harbor. Whatever the vicissitudes of politics and business, the club was a place where one could meet members of one's class with like-minded outlooks, similar interests. He walked up Rue Boissy d'Anglas and rang the bell at the massive wooden doors. He felt a wave of warmth in his chest, a certain lightness, as he anticipated meeting old friends and acquaintances.

It was early in the day, and the reception rooms were mostly empty. Richard was reading *Le Figaro* when he sensed someone coming towards him. He was disappointed—it was Michel de Clermont d'Auvergne, the son of an old friend. He would have preferred it to be the father rather than the offspring, but he smiled as they exchanged air kisses.

"May I join you," asked Michel.

"With pleasure, and how is your dear father?"

"Not so good, I'm afraid, but he's doing the best he can."

Richard reflected that he ought to visit Arnaud de Clermont d'Auvergne before it was too late.

They made small talk about the weather, the Greek and Irish economies. Michel's trade was information, and like a blue whale scooping up the krill that passed before it, he casually asked Richard, "Whatever happened with your niece's friend, what was her name?

Ever since he'd sent Michel the photos Marie-Agnès had taken, Richard wondered whether it had been wise to confide in his friend's son. Today, even members of your own class could sometimes let you down.

"Oh, you must mean Marie-Agnès. Nothing, really. She left Paris, the last I heard she was somewhere in the south. Much better weather. "

Charlotte had called him last night, asking if he could find out anything about Sauveur Paoli. Richard couldn't see how it could hurt to pick Michel's brain. *Now it's my turn.*

"Do you remember my cousin Charlotte? I know your *papa* met her several times when she was working in Paris. She's spending the winter in Marseille, where she ran into an old friend. Sauveur Paoli: does the name ring a bell?"

"I must say, Richard, you do have a knack for coming up with the strangest names! First Jacques Mornnais, and now Sauveur Paoli!"

Richard felt his excellent mood dissipate, like air escaping from a balloon.

"What about this Paoli?"

"He's a lawyer in Marseille, works in real estate."

"And…"

"Lawyer, Marseille, real estate, that's one definition of crooked. Mind you, Sauveur is a charming guy, loves sailing, but dealing with politicians, associations, developers, and all the rest, it's impossible to keep to the straight and narrow. You said he's an old friend of your cousin?"

"Yes, apparently they knew each other when they were students in Paris, but as you can imagine, that's many years ago."

Michel knew that Sauveur had been involved in radical student politics. Until he'd decided that rather than pursue his ideas about making the world a better place, he'd take the world as it was and make a better place for himself. But he said nothing more to Richard.

There was a moment of silence. Richard poured some green tea into his glass. Michel's coffee had gone cold. "This stuff tastes like cat's piss," he said as he replaced the cup on its saucer.

Richard pursed his lips; "You ought to try tea next time." He always felt that Michel was not forthcoming, holding back unknown unknowns. But he'd learn no more about Sauveur, and he turned his attention to Jacques Mornnais.

"I'm curious, what's the latest on our friend Mr. Mornnais?"

"Well, his right-hand man, Bruno Edremal, was found floating in the river Arroux, but you probably know that as it's been in the news. Apparently, he had one too many and fell in. Other than that, there's really nothing to tell."

Richard had heard Alex and Eugene talking, and he knew that Bruno had resurfaced in Lyon, very much alive but changed by his ordeal in the river. But he kept that knowledge to himself.

CHAPTER NINETEEN

December 2010

Paris

THE AIR IN THE CONFERENCE room: equal parts of tension, fear, and body odor. Patrick Trabert took a seat near the back of the room. Chances were slight that the meeting had been called to announce good news, and he wanted to leave as soon as it was over.

The meeting had been scheduled to start at three p.m. But it was not until twenty minutes later that the HR Manager, a forty-something man, entered the conference room with two young assistants in his wake. He wore one version of the middle manager's wardrobe: a dark suit, a white shirt, and a pale pink tie.

Those who had gone outside the building to smoke reappeared and took their seats, and the nervous chatter slowly died away.

"Thank you all for coming," he began.

As though we had a choice, thought Patrick. The manager's voice was calm and pleasant, cutting a path through the heavy silence, but his short, square fingers twisted a Bic *cristal* ballpoint pen. *He looks nervous, this can't be good news.*

Indeed, the HR Manager had come to deliver an all-too-familiar message. The Paris call center was not economically viable, and the operations were to be transferred to Tunisia. Of course, the bank would follow all the procedures mandated by French labor law, but it was only right to let the employees know the situation.

Patrick had been hired only last month. Didn't the company know they were moving their operations to North Africa? After his experience working in the sushi restaurant, he thought that a bank would offer more job security. Yet here he was, once again, out of work and out on his ass. Then it occurred to him that at least this time, there would be a monthly payment from the government. And of course, there was the bank account he had opened with the money his mother had stolen. Maybe things weren't so bad after all.

#   #   #

Fontainebleau

Asia Garden: red paper lanterns with gold tassels, pictures of cherry blossoms and celestial mountains, a tank with goldfish. Why was it that nothing resembled a Chinese restaurant so much as another Chinese restaurant? Still, Corinne and Sum welcomed Véronique and Patrick warmly, remembering the many times her father had walked up the street from his home to dine in their restaurant.

"Have you fixed that leak?" asked Sum.

"Oh, we're still cleaning up," smiled Véronique, "I hope you don't mind keeping our things a little longer."

"No problem, as long as you like. And what would you like to eat this evening?"

Over dishes of fried eggplant, spicy chicken, and fried rice, Patrick told Véronique about the meeting earlier that day.

"Oh?"

It sounded like she didn't want Patrick getting into the habit of expecting her to pick up the slack. Her lips collapsed into a straight line, the skin around her eyes tightened.

"But don't worry, there's always my unemployment to tide me over," he said. A weak, *lets-make-the-best-of-it* smile: "I guess so."

He could have told Véronique how he'd managed to transfer his mother's ill-gotten gains into a bank account in Jersey. He hadn't stolen the funds; he'd just moved them to a safer place. But to an outsider, it might have sounded like the money had again been misappropriated, so he didn't mention the Jersey bank account to her.

CHAPTER TWENTY

Alexandria, Virginia

EUGENE HAD NEVER BEEN GOOD at small talk, and as of late, whenever Kate asked him anything, his responses were, more often than not, "Yes," "No," and "Perhaps." It didn't make for scintillating conversation. He would be flying back to France tomorrow, and she hoped that he would straighten out whatever was eating at him.

#   #   #

Lyon

The New York Times had started to publish the U.S. diplomatic cables provided by Wikileaks, furnishing ample reading material as Eugene waited for his flight. Hours later, when he landed in Paris, it was still dark; at this time of the year, daybreak was hours away. While waiting for his connecting flight, he killed some more time reading about Cablegate. Reflecting how dangerous it could be to put things in writing, and how nearly impossible it was to avoid doing so.

The weather in Lyon was even more unpleasant than in Paris: colder, windier, damper. The gloomy clouds hung just above his head, and he had to keep reminding himself that Lyon was only a stopping off point on his way to skiing in the Alps. But his mood changed when he arrived at Travis and Julie's home in the late afternoon. Julie had started cooking dinner. He wasn't sure what it was, but it smelled delicious. Their apartment was light and bright, and it occurred to him how much more at home he now felt in France than in Washington. Even with the lousy weather.

Sitting around with Travis and Julie, Eugene felt warm and at ease as they sipped Kirs and chatted about their upcoming ski holiday. But happy images of the snowy mountains couldn't stifle his feeling of regret. Regret at how cold he'd been when he'd called Alex a few days ago, regret that he hadn't dared to ask her about the painting at Trubenne. Why the fuck had he avoided having that conversation? Eugene was angry with himself for the way he had acted. He wasn't a child anymore, and he had been behaving childishly. When he had some privacy, he'd call her, apologize for his behavior and see when they could meet.

#   #   #

Eugene and Travis were sitting in the living room, discussing Cablegate, when Eugene felt a whirring in his pocket, like a muted dentist's drill: his cell phone was vibrating. He looked at the screen, saw it was Alex, got up and excused himself, walked into the hallway, eager to tell her that they needed to meet.

"I've been trying to reach you."

"Oh, I've been traveling, I left D.C., and I'm in Lyon right now. With the people I stayed with last year. We're going skiing in a couple of days."

"How lucky for you. Look, I don't want to keep you from your friends…"

"Oh, that's okay, how are you?"

"Fine, fine. I just wanted to tell you that when we spoke last week, I forgot to mention that I'd seen Bruno, he's in Marseille." She recounted her run-in with Bruno, and added, "I just thought that you might want to know."

He was silent for a moment, looking for the words to tell her that he needed to see her. Then Julie walked into the hallway, the words got caught in his throat, and instead, he thanked her, said he'd be in touch.

\#   \#   \#

A few days later, Eugene was alone in the apartment: Julie was out shopping, and it was Travis' last day at work. Privacy, silence: *let's do it.* He had started to call Alex when Julie burst into the apartment, carrying two bags of groceries to take to their chalet. "Hey Eugene," she called out as the bags dropped to the floor—it was not the right time to talk to Alex.

\#   \#   \#

Alex's phone rang once before the call was disconnected. She saw Eugene's name flash on the screen and waited for him to call back. When he did not, she concluded that he was playing a game whose rules were unknown to her.

\#   \#   \#

Fuck. Eugene picked up the bags of groceries and carried them into the kitchen. It was too complicated to have a serious conversation with Alex, with Julie and Travis popping in and out—it was their apartment, after all. It would be easier to find some time alone when they were at La Clusaz, and he decided to call Alex then.

CHAPTER TWENTY-ONE

Lyon

JACQUES STARED AT THE BACK of his chauffeur's shaved head, round like an egg at the top, flat at the bottom where it connected to his thick neck. He'd hired him when a stupid kid, high on drugs, had driven his motorcycle into the windshield of the van that his chauffeur Tarek was driving. He regretted losing Tarek, who knew what he wanted before he'd said a word. But the new man, Charles-Antoine Nasri, seemed to be working out. Jacques expelled air from his nostrils a bit more forcefully as he thought, not for the first time: what kind of a name was Charles-Antoine for an Arab? Yes, Arabs made the best drivers: they were good mechanics, were glad to have work and behaved themselves. Not like the French, not like Bruno, who was smart but who drank too much. And who knew too much.

He unfolded the morning edition of *Le Figaro*. The world was going to hell in a handbasket, so nothing new there. He smirked as he thought about the American President Obama: with all his fine talk about change, there he was in bed with Goldman Sachs. Not that that bothered Jacques, quite the contrary. Next was the French President, Bill Palmac, a tightly wound spring with an authoritarian streak. But the French government needed uranium for its reactors, and the rest didn't matter. He made a note to remember to stop referring to the President as 'Bonsai Bill.'

In a short while, he would be meeting with the investors from Brezikstan, who had bought the luxury hotel, the Pavillon de la Roche. Brezikstan was home to large deposits of uranium ore, and the country's rulers, as well as Jacques, had grown rich on the sale of uranium to France. The business had gone so well that they had asked Jacques to explore other investment opportunities in France, and that had led to the purchase of the Pavillon de la Roche.

They were nearing Lyon when he turned to the newspaper's *Gastronomie* section, and his eye fell upon a review of a new restaurant in that city: Chez Blondie. The restaurant was a fresh, modern take on the traditional Lyonnais "*Bouchon*," said the reviewer. The 'Brekis' were always eager to try whatever was the trendiest, the most popular. He was sure that they'd appreciate a trip to Chez Blondie. When Jacques arrived at the hotel, he asked the concierge to make a reservation for lunch there later in the week.

#   #   #

The six men were seated three abreast at a table at the far end of the dining room. Jacques, his back to the mural, was deep in discussion with the Brezikstan Finance Minister when the latter lifted his head and looked up past Jacques's shoulder. "My dear Jacques," he said, "I didn't know you had peasant ancestors, I always thought your origins were most aristocratic."

Jacques was indeed the offspring of Portuguese peasants, but he had long ago changed both his name and his biography. Two pink spots appeared on his cheeks as he willed himself to remain calm.

"Pardon me?"

The finance minister chuckled, "Look at that mural behind you. The fellow at the end of the table on the right, he looks exactly like you, my friend."

Jacques twisted around, stood up to get a better look, and, in a rare occurrence for him, shivered. Tarek, Bruno, Mila, even the red-haired cow— there they were along with his own likeness and a few unknown faces.

63

"Well, yes, I must admit, it's a remarkable resemblance." His pulse had quickened: what the fuck was going on? Who but Li or Wen could have done a mural in the unmistakable style of Le Nain Frères with those faces?

Marie-Agnès had been on the lookout for the group from Brezikstan. A wave of fear rolled over her when she saw Jacques enter Chez Blondie. Yet she was not surprised; she had been expecting him to show up one day. But Mag wasn't ready to meet Jacques; she slipped quickly back into the kitchen, where she and Tomas agreed that he would be the one to approach the group at the end of their meal.

The finance minister had launched into a monologue describing the different factions in the Brezikstan governing elite. Jacques tried to follow the thread of his luncheon companion's discourse, but anxiety gnawed at his innards. This was not the meal he had been looking forward to. The finance minister was staring at him, waiting for Jacques to comment on something he'd just said. "Yes, indeed," was all that Jacques could manage; it was as though he had a mouthful of dental plaster.

At the end of the meal, Tomas came over to their table. The Brekis were lavish with their praise; they even asked to take their photo with Tomas. The finance minister pointed to the mural: "Don't you think that the man there on the right looks just like our friend?" Tomas feigned surprise, "I would not have noticed, but you could be right."

Jacques spoke for the first time: "May I ask you for the name of the artist?"

"Of course, you may," he replied, "But I'm afraid I can't help you there. We hired some Polish painters to renovate the place, and one of them offered to paint a mural for us. Paid them in cash," he shook his head, "You know how these posted workers are, here today, gone tomorrow. I have no idea where they might be now."

Jacques glared at him. A menacing look—the stocky man with twinkling gray eyes was lying— and an unspoken question: who had painted the bloody mural, and why?

Unfazed and still smiling, Tomas moved on to greet the diners at the adjoining tables. Over the past months, a bond of trust had grown between him and Marie-Agnès. In the end, she had told her companion the whole story. A story that started with the day, a little over a year ago, when she had run into Alex in Parc Monceau on her way to a job interview at Jacques's magazine *Artixia*. Tomas had despised Jacques Mornnais long before he met him. It pleased him to think that he had been a small source of discomfort to that amoral and avaricious man.

CHAPTER TWENTY-TWO

Marseille

THE SUN WAS NOT YET up when Bruno let himself into the building on Rue Saint-Jacques and climbed the steps to the second floor two at a time to reach Sauveur Paoli's office. An early riser, the lawyer was already at work when Bruno rang the bell. Sauveur was seated at a large table. On either side, rows of folders were piled so high that the slightest movement threatened to set off an avalanche of paper. He picked a thick file from the top of one of the paper mountains and handed it to Bruno.

"Here, have a look. These are all people who owe me money. I've been too busy to chase after them, and I'd like you to remind them that I'm expecting to be paid." He laughed, "After all, I'm not the Red Cross."

"Yeah, otherwise, they might be needing some medical attention."

"No need for that, Bruno, just remind them politely that they need to settle their bills. I'm sure they'll understand."

Times had changed. A few decades earlier, the lawyer would have been shouting, threatening dire consequences. Now, with the dusting of silver in his hair and his well-fitting suit, he was calm, self-assured: it would be sufficient to mention his name and request payment.

Bruno sat at a smaller, uncluttered table in front of a window overlooking the courtyard. Come spring, there would be a sea of green, but for now, the trees were mostly bare, giving the place a look of desolation. He leafed through the folder. The clients were real estate agencies, property developers, a trade association, all in Marseille.

The last file was for a title search done for another lawyer, this time in Paris: Mervin R. Peters. There was something familiar about that name; then, he remembered the heavyset lawyer to whom Jacques had sold so many fakes. Once, they had even stolen one of the paintings and sold him another to replace it.

"I know this guy, the lawyer. I met him while I was working for Jacques Mornnais."

Sauveur looked up: "Oh, Merv Peters? Well, good, I'm sure he'll be happy to hear from you."

#   #   #

Bruno took the files into a tiny room, no bigger than a walk-in closet. There was a single window, caked over with dirt. The window faced an airshaft that was home to a flock of pigeons. Bruno felt so irritated by the racket the pigeons made, cooing and flapping their wings, that he felt an urge to kill them. The urge passed, and he started to make his calls.

He had had to call back several times before reaching most of the clients. But when he did contact them, as Sauveur had suggested, mentioning his name elicited a promise to settle the bill immediately. He thanked them and couldn't resist adding that if they hadn't received payment in a week, he'd be happy to stop by to pick up the check.

Merv Peters was finishing breakfast at La Belle Fermière when his cell phone buzzed. "Paoli" flashed on the screen. What could the lawyer want, he wondered, and then he remembered that he hadn't paid his bill. Paoli had sent his men around to Nicolas Pagès's house twice. He'd even arranged for Merv to visit the house himself, all to no avail: Nicolas Pagès's files were not in the house. Still, Merv knew he had to pay the bill, but the call could wait until he returned to his office—he was not about to start discussing his problem in front of everyone.

Bruno tried Merv's cell phone again, left a message for him at his office, and called again. His perseverance paid off when, at the end of the morning, Merv's secretary put his call through.

"*Maître* Peters?" The man spoke softly, his tone vaguely menacing. Merv wondered where he'd heard that voice before.

"Yes...." He said as he tried to match the voice to a name or a face.

"I'm calling from *Maître* Paoli's office. We know it's probably just an oversight, but *Maître* Paoli would appreciate you settling his invoice."

"Yes, of course, I'm terribly sorry. So busy, I'm sure you understand. I'll attend to it immediately Mr.? I didn't catch your name."

"Edremal, Bruno Edremal. I believe we've met before, I used to work for Jacques Mornnais."

Now it came back to him. Merv remembered Bruno Edremal—a big man with a low, calm voice. Its insinuation of violence inspired a feeling of dread: for Merv, he was worse than Jacques.

"Br...Bruno? I'm sorry, but I had heard that you were in um, an accident?"

"You mean that I was dead? Well, it looks like I've come back from the dead, doesn't it? Anyhow, I'll tell *Maître* Paoli that you'll be putting a check in the mail. It's been nice talking to you."

The call ended, and Merv Peters rushed to the toilet before he soiled himself.

CHAPTER TWENTY-THREE

CHRISTMAS LIGHTS TWINKLED IN THE December night. It took Sauveur a half an hour to walk home from his office, but he enjoyed the exercise. His house, visible from the highway, was something of a landmark. Painted pale yellow, the color of dried wheat, the Villa des Deux Vents sat on a rocky outcrop below the Corniche. The previous owner, an architect, had carved out a swimming pool at the tip of the rock. It was a spectacular setting and totally illegal. When Sauveur bought the Villa des Deux Vents, there were rumblings from environmental activists that the house ought to be torn down, and the swimming pool opened to the public. But as Sauveur had friends in the right places, he petitioned for and was granted an exemption from the law that protected the waterfront from the construction of private dwellings.

He was in a perfect mood. One of the curators from Marseille's Musée Burlotti was coming to view the painting by Paul Signac, which he had bought several months before. Sauveur hadn't been able to resist bragging about his purchase to some friends; word had gotten around, and now the museum was considering including it in the exhibition of Pointillist painters it was organizing. Jacques Mornnais, his art consultant, had assured him that this was one of Signac's finest works. It had been in a private collection for many years and had only recently come on the market.

Stéphanie Amelinni sipped her champagne, looking up at Sauveur through lashes thick with black mascara. She crossed her legs and hoped that he would notice her shapely limbs. It had been such a stroke of luck. She'd been working in an art gallery on Rue Sainte when the assistant curator job at the Burlotti had come vacant. There had been nothing to distinguish Stéphanie from the other candidates. Except that her uncle had touted her merits to some of his pals. That was how things worked: friends helped each other. And now, here she was, meeting a very charming man who didn't appear to have a wife or a companion. The situation was ripe with possibilities. If only she could have come alone.

#   #   #

Sitting next to Stephanie on the sofa was Maud Cousin, an older woman with legs like tree trunks, with not even a hint of mascara on her pale blond eyelashes. Maud had worked at the museum for over a decade. When the assistant curator job had become available, she thought that her time had come. Yet she had been passed over for the job. Even the Ayala champagne could not take away the bitterness in her mouth.

Below the living room, a lush garden—succulents, shrubs, and palm trees— surrounded the path leading to the swimming pool, "Oh, how beautiful" Stéphanie gushed as Sauveur turned on the outdoor lights. *If I weren't here, she'd probably be in bed with him already,* mused Maud.

"I assume that is the painting you wish to lend us." She pointed to the Signac that hung on the living room wall. Sauveur caught the edge in her voice, "Yes, Madame, it would be an honor for me," giving her his full attention.

"It's so, so beautiful." Stéphanie had not yet mastered artspeak.

Maud's pale lashes fluttered: "I don't believe we were aware of this painting."

"It was in a private collection for many years. I'll be happy to provide you with proof of provenance."

"Oh, that would be great," said Stéphanie.

"A private collection?" Maud pursed her lips: "Has this painting been authenticated by an expert?"

"Yes, I believe my art consultant took care of that. I remember him telling me it was one of the finest Signacs that he'd ever seen. As I said, I'll send you all the documents in my possession."

They had some more champagne, Sauveur effortlessly guiding the conversation through the cloud of small talk until Maud stood up. "Thank you so much. Please do send us your information."

#   #   #

An autopsy of the evening:

Stéphanie was delighted to have met Sauveur; he had been so charming. As she left the pale-yellow house, she imagined herself standing with him at the exhibition's opening, with the grouchy Maud nowhere in sight.

Maud had found the evening tiring. She had to admit that Sauveur was an attractive man, but what was Stéphanie thinking about? Certainly not the museum's reputation! A newly discovered Signac? Perhaps, but she would believe it when she saw the proof and not before. She imagined herself at the exhibition's opening: neither Stéphanie nor Sauveur was in the picture.

As for Sauveur, he wondered if he had paid enough attention to Maud Cousin. Business first.

#   #   #

Maud called Sauveur a few days later.

"Ah, Madame Cousin, so nice to hear from you."

"I'm calling about your painting, Mr. Paoli. We've reviewed the documents you sent over. They say that "Marina at Saint-Malo" came from a private collection, but there is no name."

"Yes, I know. My advisor told me that the family wanted to remain very discreet."

"I understand. My problem is that Marina at Saint-Malo purports to be a lost work, and we really need to know more about how it came into your possession. I see that Mr. Nicolas Pagès established a certificate of authenticity. With your permission, I'd like to contact him to see if he can help us."

"No problem, by all means, please do. I paid a small fortune for that painting, so it has to be the real thing." As he said this, Sauveur realized that quite the opposite might be true: he had paid a small fortune for something that was not the real deal. Seeking reassurance, he called Jacques Mornnais.

CHAPTER TWENTY-FOUR

Château d'Hélène

JACQUES LOOKED AT THE CALENDAR. It was already December, and he still had no plans for the Christmas holiday. Of course, he would go away, no one that he knew stayed home at this time of the year, but Mila had always taken care of the reservations. For a while, he surfed the internet aimlessly, then with a sigh, called his travel agent. He would go to Singapore as usual to see his lawyers. Afterward, he would fly to Montenegro and check on the paintings he had shipped to his warehouse there last spring when he'd been having some trouble with the American.

Jacques scowled, ruminating about how the American had outmaneuvered him. His cell phone started to vibrate: 'Merv' flashed on the screen. *Merde.* There was no point in avoiding the annoying lawyer; he would just keep calling until Jacques answered.

"Yes."

"Hi Jacques, it's me."

"Yes, I know that, Merv. How can I help?"

"Well, actually, I have some news that might interest you."

"Oh, really."

"Yeah. Do you know a lawyer in Marseille, by the name of Sauveur Paoli?"

"Hmm, sounds familiar. Why do you ask?"

"Well, guess who's working for him?"

"Will you stop asking me questions and get to the point?" he snapped.

"Your man Bruno, the one who drowned. Well, he's quite alive. Did you know that?" Without waiting for a reply, he went on, "He called me the other day about a bill I owe Sauveur. We had a nice chat, he said he'd come back from the dead."

Silence. "Jacques, are you there?"

"Yes, he called me a while ago. In fact, I had lunch with him."

"I just thought you might want to know. And Jacques, while we're talking, remember, I mentioned that I was thinking about selling my collection?"

"Yes."

"Well, I'm going to go ahead and do it. I thought since you and Nicolas helped me to acquire the paintings, you could help me to sell them. What do you think? I mean, you said he had all the records, but the last time we spoke, you also said you'd check if you had any information on their provenance. I was hoping that you might since you advised me to purchase them."

Merv paused, and when Jacques remained silent, he continued. "I know how busy you are, and maybe you don't have time for me. Now that Nicholas is dead, I guess I could go to some other dealers, have them research the provenance—there are certainly enough to go around in Paris."

"No need to do that, my friend. Of course, I'll do my best to help you. But can it wait until the New Year? In a week, no one will be around."

"Sure, Jacques, I knew I could count on you. Well, have a happy holiday, if we don't speak before the New Year."

Jacques' mood was as bleak as the landscape outside the windows: a gray sky barely lit by the winter sun, dark, bare trees, vegetation shriveled by the cold. It was just as well that Merv Peters had called. He didn't like the idea of Bruno working for Sauveur—who knew what they had discussed—but at least now he knew where to find him. As for Merv Peters, the man was starting to piss him off. His eyes darkened as his lips collapsed into a thin line. Had Bruno been there, he would have known what that meant.

A buzzing sound interrupted his thoughts: Sauveur's name flashed on the screen. *Putain,* he'd had enough for one day, and he let the phone ring until Sauveur hung up without leaving a message.

CHAPTER TWENTY-FIVE

Marseille

THE WINTER SKY, SWEPT CLEAR BY days of wind, was a deep, brilliant blue. A lone white cloud floated overhead. Sauveur and Charlotte drove to the marina at La Pointe Rouge and boarded the motorboat his friend kept moored there. The port was as packed with boats as a supermarket parking lot on a Saturday morning. Most of the vessels left the marina less than three times a year, evidence of the gap between the dreams of many of their owners to lead a sporting life, and the reality of doing it.

Sauveur, however, was an accomplished sailor. He steered the boat expertly out of the crowded harbor and headed first in the direction of the Vieux Port.

"I love to see the Vieux Port from the sea," he said to her, "It's a totally different perspective from that of the tourists in the waterfront cafés, drinking beer and eating crepes."

Charlotte had not sounded too keen on the maritime excursion, but in the end, she had agreed to join him. Now that she was onboard, Sauveur could see her smiling as they approached the Vieux Port, passing between Fort Saint-Nicolas on the one side and Fort-Saint-Jean on the other. He then turned and returned to the open sea, heading south along the coast.

They passed the Vallon des Auffes. The iconic bridge and the restaurant where they had dined came into view. The little village did indeed look different when approached from the sea. At Callalongue, the Calanques' majestic craggy white peaks rose from the sea. They had probably not changed much since the Greeks, the Turks, and then the Romans sailed to Marseille. At Sormiou, Sauveur guided the boat into a little bay and dropped anchor. Warmed by the midday sun, they snacked on sandwiches. Sauveur opened a bottle of wine.

"This is so magnificent, it takes my breath away."

"Yes, I thought you might enjoy discovering the Calanques, I like to come here and just feel the peacefulness and the silence."

Charlotte took a sip of wine, "Yes, we're a long way from Montmartre, aren't we?"

"Indeed. We had some good times. And believe it or not, I'm still in touch with some of the guys I knew then. They're all upstanding members of the community, just like me." He smiled. "But I sometimes wonder whatever became of that American, the guy who backed out."

"Do you really care? It was so long ago."

"I guess not, and anyway, I've got more important things to think about." They were now standing leaning against the railing. Sauveur rested an arm on Charlotte's shoulder: "I bought a painting last summer, a beautiful painting by Paul Signac. I paid a lot of money for it, and it turns out it may be a fake. I'm not too happy about that."

Signac, hadn't Alex been talking about a painting by Paul Signac? Leave it alone. She smiled, "Well, I hope you can sort things out with your painting."

"Me too," and he pulled her towards him and kissed her. It was a delicious kiss that brought Charlotte back to her three small rooms in Montmartre. The familiar warm feeling that she'd missed for so many years returned, only to be stifled when a loud whistle resounded, followed by clapping and cheering. They hadn't noticed the groups of boys sunning themselves on a ledge of the calanque. Sauveur laughed, "Why don't we continue this conversation someplace a bit more private?" They corked the bottle, put the rubbish in a plastic bag, and headed back to La Pointe Rouge and then to the pale-yellow house below the Corniche.

CHAPTER TWENTY-SIX

Fontainebleau

IT HAD TAKEN THE LABOR union only a few days to organize the strike. The marchers carried signs that proclaimed, 'Don't Ship Our Jobs Overseas,' there was a table with hot coffee, tea, and croissants to keep their spirits up. Television crews were filming the demonstration. A journalist, attracted by Patrick's scruffy, handsome look, thrust a microphone in his face. He mumbled something about management's unfair, yes, even immoral decision. He hung around for a while until the cameras were gone and then slipped away to return to Fontainebleau.

He lifted the bottle of beer to his lips: "I wanna get out of here," he said to Véronique. She sighed and put down her sandwich. The filling—industrial-strength mayonnaise with something purporting to be tuna fish—had seen better days, and the bread stuck in her throat like a lump of soggy newspaper.

She counted on the fingers of her out-stretched hand: "Aigues-Mortes, Marseille, Paris, Fontainebleau, and now you wanna go someplace else? You've got to stop running. Find another job. Stay in one place."

"Christmas is coming, it's no time to look for work. We both know that nothing will happen before the New Year. Meantime, I can't stand this gray weather anymore—I need to see the sun. Let's go down to Marseille, stay in your house there, and I promise to look for work when we get back in January."

Véronique was starting to get tired of Patrick. Okay, it had been fun in the beginning, but now he was like a mussel, attached firmly to a rock—a rock named Véronique. December was such a depressing month: the short days, the dark mornings, the sun setting in the late afternoon. With the approach of Christmas, her mood turned black. And it didn't help that every time she sold an object, it reminded her of her father's gruesome murder. Perhaps a trip south would be a good idea. But at the right moment, she'd tell him that it was over. Patrick had a friend in Marseille, she knew that. So, he would have a place to stay. And let him ask his mother for money, it wouldn't be the first time, she suspected.

"Okay, maybe you're right. I've been running on empty these past weeks, I think a rest would do me good."

#   #   #

Patrick looked at her as she chewed on the tasteless sandwich. Her dull hair was pulled back into a messy ponytail, the first traces of two thin lines had appeared, running from her nose to her lips, she had deep circles under her eyes. She looked a lot less attractive than the girl who had caught him spying on the house last July. It was time to move on. He could stay with David in Marseille, look for work there. He'd have his unemployment benefits, and of course, there was always the bank account in Jersey if he needed funds to tide him over.

Their decisions taken, they drove south.

#   #   #

Her face brown and wrinkled as an overripe berry, Caroline wheeled her small suitcase through Zaventem airport. The flight from Phuket to Brussels had been exhausting. She'd spent over fifteen hours in economy class—and now, it felt good to be able to walk, get the blood circulating in her legs. Caroline was happy living in Phuket, her job in the bookstore a pleasant change from the dreary back office of Alpine Trading Bank. And the sun. Perhaps she'd overdone it a bit, but after a lifetime of fighting the elements—the wind, the rain, and the cold—the constant mild weather lifted her spirits from the pavement up to the sky.

The only cloud on the horizon—and it was a big, black cloud—was her son Patrick. Or, more precisely, the fact that he had stolen the money she had worked so carefully to embezzle. The money had been in dormant accounts, and Caroline saw it not as theft, but more as an equitable redistribution of assets.

That Patrick had taken the notion of redistribution one step further infuriated her. He was a snake in the grass—he had betrayed her trust. She checked into a cheap hotel near Gare du Midi, slept all day until she boarded a bus for Marseille that evening. The bus arrived at the terminal at noon the following day. Caroline splurged and took a taxi to Traverse Paul. She didn't imagine that Patrick would be there; it was an excellent place to rest up and start looking for him.

The door in the wall was ajar. Caroline tried to recall whether the lock had been forced when she departed in a hurry last September. *Well, no matter, I'm here now, and that's what counts.* Cautiously, she stepped inside, carrying her little suitcase up the gravel walk that ran alongside the house. As she crossed the lawn to look for the key that she'd left under a large ceramic pot outside the kitchen entrance, Patrick chanced to gaze out of the living room windows.

CHAPTER TWENTY-SEVEN

Marseille

IT WAS EARLY MORNING, AND Sauveur was on his way to work. Across from the Catalans beach, he stood at the counter of the Welcome Café, watched two seagulls soaring and diving over the placid blue sea. It was strange, how at peace he felt, how incredible it was to have found Charlotte after all these years. Was he in love with her? All he knew for sure was that he felt a warm tingle, a lightness, for the first time in years. Charlotte was not as slender as she had been, but then again, neither was he, and did it really matter now? She told him how much she had enjoyed their little outing. She and her niece Alex were going to Paris for the Christmas holiday, and he promised to take them both to the Frioul islands when they returned in January.

A dazzling day, the Mediterranean in winter, as it should be: a slight breeze, a cloudless sky, and brilliant sunshine. Sauveur enjoyed walking so much that he decided to take the longer route to his office, passing by the Pharo Garden. He skirted the Vieux Port, packed as always with boats that almost never left their berths. The waterfront was deserted—it was too early for the herds of tourists. He smelled the sea, and as he neared Rue Breteuil, the odor of the fish market on Quai des Belges tickled his nostrils.

He turned onto Rue Saint-Jacques. The stately buildings needed a good cleaning, but Marseille was a poor city—unlike Paris, where owners had to clean their buildings' facades every ten years. But despite the grime, it was worth taking the time to admire the elegant nineteenth-century wooden doors at the entrance to each edifice. Such were his thoughts as he climbed the stairs to his office.

A phone call from Merv Peters took his mind off architecture and back to the present.

"I hope you've received my check."

"Yes, thank you." He'd never met the man, tried to imagine what he looked like. "I'm sorry we couldn't find what you were looking for."

"Well, that's just it. I was wondering if you couldn't ask someone to take a thorough look. The last time, I felt rushed, and I cannot believe that all the documents have just disappeared."

"Can you tell me, what are these documents that you're so obsessed with?"

"It's quite simple. The owner of the house was an art dealer who sold me many of the paintings in my collection. I may sell some of those paintings, and I need proof of provenance. The documents were not in his gallery in Fontainebleau, so they must be at the house in Marseille. But that's not all. In October, this guy, Nicolas Pagès, turned up dead, his throat slit from ear to ear. It sounds pretty horrific. So, you can see why I'm a bit stressed, or obsessed, as you say, about all of this."

Nicolas Pagès. Sauveur had told Maud Cousins to feel free to contact the expert who had authenticated his painting: the same Nicolas Pagès. This wasn't going to happen, and he found himself in the same situation as Merv, looking for proof of the provenance of the Signac.

Sauveur thought back to the men he had sent with Merv the last time: could they have overlooked something, missed a hiding place? He doubted it, but he'd ask Bruno to go to Traverse Paul. If there were any records there, Bruno would find them. And Merv would pay for his time.

Another thought occurred to him: "How did you happen to meet Nicolas Pagès?"

"My art consultant, a man named Jacques Mornnais, introduced me to him. Why do you ask? Do you know Jacques?"

"No, not really, although I think I've heard his name mentioned. Isn't he the one who publishes the magazine, *Artixia*?"

"Yeah, one and the same."

"Tell me something, did you ask this Mornnais guy about your documents?"

Merv sighed. "Yeah, he said he'd try to help, but so far it looks like Nicolas had everything. So, I'm in the shit, big time."

"I see. About your documents, they could be someplace else, or maybe they have disappeared entirely. Surely that must have occurred to you."

"Yes, of course it has. But I'd like it if you could take one last look for me."

"Well then, leave it with me."

Sauveur left his office and walked back to the Pharo garden. He sat on a bench overlooking the entrance to the Vieux Port, where he had taken Charlotte a few days ago. It was just as well that Jacques hadn't taken his call the other day. He would wait to see to hear back from Maud Cousins. If she continued to question the authenticity of his Signac, he knew what he had to do.

CHAPTER TWENTY-EIGHT

Neuilly-sur-Seine

RICHARD'S HOUSEKEEPER MARIA HAD ORDERED a Christmas tree, a stately evergreen that had been delivered that afternoon. She led Alex and Charlotte down to the basement, where the three women rummaged through boxes of decorations that Chloe had collected over the years. They picked out an assortment of gold and silver ornaments, brought them up to the apartment and set about decorating the tree as the fresh smell of the pine needles filled the living room.

Despite the fun of decorating the tree, Charlotte could sense that Alex was as gloomy as a one-star hotel. She felt that some comfort food was in order. Dinner consisted of creamy duck liver pâté, slivers of salami, and deviled eggs, followed by veal birds in a tomato and wine sauce, with noodles and peas. Alex perked up a bit, but Charlotte was not sure if that was due to the food or the Morgon she washed it down with.

Richard dug into a scooped-out pineapple shell and heaped a mixture of fruit and ice cream into his dish. "So, Charlotte, how is your friend Sauveur?"

"As far as I know, he's fine. But you've stolen my line—I was going to ask you if you had any news about him."

Richard chewed slowly on a piece of pineapple, savoring the combination of the fruit and the vanilla ice cream, then wiped his lips.

"In fact, I have quite a bit of news, my dear cousin. First, I spoke to Michel de Clermont d'Auvergne. If my memory serves me, he said, and I quote: 'Lawyer, Marseille, real estate, that's one definition of crooked.' "

Two roses bloomed in Charlotte's cheeks. Richard slurped another spoonful of fruit and continued: "The trouble with Michel, he's not like his father. I always have the feeling he's holding back on me, it's so disappointing. So, I decided to make my own inquiries elsewhere." He paused, enjoying the dessert and the women's attention.

"A young man, well, actually he's not that young any more. I trained him years ago when I was running our bank…" Charlotte and Alex waited patiently for Richard to get to the point. "He's now President of the Marseille International Credit Bank. And as he says, Marseille is really a small city— there are only five hundred people that one absolutely needs to know. But I'm getting ahead of myself. I thought he might shed some light on your friend Sauveur, so I called him. And he knew whom I was talking about right off the bat. One of the five hundred, you see. There were some shall-we-say youthful indiscretions—but you probably know about that, Charlotte. Then, he married into an old land-owning family based in La Ciotat, which is just outside of Marseille. Sauveur himself comes from a family of jurists— lawyers and judges—so being a real estate lawyer was only natural. It would seem that in Marseille, everything depends on whom you know. I guess that's not too different from Paris, is it? And your friend Sauveur appears to have relationships with, well, let's call it a diverse group of people. I'm sorry to say this Charlotte, but Michel's take seems to be spot-on."

"And his wife in all of this?" asked Alex.

"Oh, I forgot about that. She passed away some time ago, and Sauveur inherited the property that she had brought to the party. No children, sad to say."

Charlotte played with a chunk of pineapple, trying to slide it onto her spoon. "I can't say I'm too surprised, Richard. But here's something I'll bet your friend doesn't know, not yet anyway. Sauveur bought a painting that he now thinks is a fake, and guess who sold it to him? That's right,

Jacques Mornnais."

"Oh, really? Mr. Mornnais came up in my conversation with Michel as well. First, he asked about your friend, Marie-Agnès, and I told him she was off traveling someplace. Then he told me that Bruno Edremal had drowned. I wonder if he was testing me to see if I knew that Bruno was alive, or if he really believed he was dead. Anyway, I said nothing."

It was Alex's turn to blush. She turned to Charlotte. "That reminds me, there's something I forgot to tell you." She recounted how Bruno had pulled her out of the bushes in the Pierre Puget garden.

"And, as I was walking home, I saw him again, on Rue Saint-Jacques. He came out of the building where your friend Sauveur Paoli and some other lawyers have their offices. But I have no idea what he was doing there."

"How interesting! Why didn't you mention that before?"

"I don't know, it just slipped my mind." Alex didn't tell Charlotte that she had been preoccupied, thinking about Eugene. She thought about him again; she saw the warm brown eyes flecked with gold. When she'd told him about seeing Bruno, he'd practically hung up on her. She just didn't get it.

CHAPTER TWENTY-NINE

Marseille

HE RODE THE MOTORCYCLE ALONG the Corniche, enjoyed the feeling of the bike's power between his legs, but didn't speed. He paid attention to the traffic—the Marseillais were fucking crazy drivers, that was for sure. And besides, he was working, this was no pleasure outing.

Bruno had been surprised when Sauveur explained what he wanted him to do. Nicolas Pagès was dead, so normally the house would be empty. Sauveur's client was sure that Pagès had kept records of sales in the house. The client had already visited the house with one of Sauveur's assistants, and they had found nothing. But perhaps they had not looked closely enough. That was Bruno's job: to take a good, thorough look. However, if there was anyone in the house, he was not to go in. Was Bruno clear on that?

"Yes, boss, understood. But what do I do if I find the records?"

"Call me, and we'll take it from there."

Sauveur hadn't asked him if he knew Nicolas Pagès; therefore, he felt no need to say that he had known him quite well. If asked about it later, Bruno could simply say that he didn't remember, that was one of the useful things about his accident. Indeed, there were still a few things that he couldn't remember. The problem was that he didn't know what they were: unknown unknowns. They were like deep, black holes. But they were not empty—it was just that he couldn't see what was there. Well, with time, he'd fill in those holes, as he'd managed to fill in all the rest.

Traverse Paul was deserted. The bare tree branches rustled in the wind, illuminated by dim overhead lights. Bruno kept to the shadows as he coasted silently up the road until he came to number 89. He turned the bike around, leaned it up against the wall opposite the house, ready for a quick departure if necessary.

The door in the wall was ajar. Had the lock been tampered with? As he walked up the path that ran alongside the house, he thought back to his last meeting with Nicolas Pagès. It was just before his accident last January, when the art dealer had returned 'Storm Over the Sea' to him, along with his certificate of authenticity. Bruno's mind lurched back to his last night at Jacques' château. He had kept the painting with him while he ate dinner, then he had blacked out, and the next thing he knew, he had been thrown him into the river Arroux—it was a miracle that he had survived. He saw a man shivering violently from the cold, crawl out of the river, his stiff fingers clawing the mud as he moved up the riverbank. Overhead, two seagulls screeched, bringing him back to the present moment.

As he stood staring at the house, the wind carried the sound of voices across the lawn. Sauveur had said not to enter the house if anyone was there. But he hadn't said anything about not trying to identify them. An enormous plane tree stood near the house; its trunk would shield him as he tried to look inside. Creeping across the lawn, he positioned himself behind the tree. Plate glass windows stretched across the length of the dimly lit living room. He saw three people: a young man, a woman who could be his sister or his companion, and a much older woman. They were arguing; the man paced back and forth, his eyes cast downward as the older woman yelled at him. The younger woman, who sat on a sofa, picked at her fingernails, and said nothing.

No one was looking out the window. Bruno took a chance and moved out from behind the tree and into the shadows. He could see the threesome more distinctly now: the older woman, deeply tanned, whose short hair

looked as if it had been run through by an electric current; the young man…
Bruno felt a twinge of excitement: it was the kid he had roughed up a few
months ago. The voices were clearer now: the older woman was screaming:
"You had no right to take my money, Patrick,"

"I'm sorry, mother, that you feel that way. I did it for your own good."

The girl looked up from her hands just as Bruno stepped back behind
the plane tree.

"I've had enough of this shit, I'm going to bed." She turned and climbed
the stairs to the first floor.

It had been an accident, but he'd found Caroline Trabert. Sandra was
expecting him to get her a share of Caroline's money, but what could he do
now? Sauveur had said not to go inside if the house wasn't empty, and he
didn't want to risk pissing him off. Thinking about Sandra in Lyon reminded
him of the American he had met there. Eugene had tried to help him once,
and maybe he would do it again. Bruno was sure he had his reasons. Eugene
was not the sort to do something in a disinterested way.

#   #   #

Véronique happened to look down at the street as she was closing the
shutters to her bedroom window. A man walked his motorcycle partway
down the road, and then he sped off into the night. She was upset with both
Patrick and Caroline: being a thief seemed to run in the family. The sooner
they were both out of her life, the better. She wondered where the man on
the motorcycle had come from. And then the thought dissolved as she went
to sleep with other problems on her mind.

CHAPTER THIRTY

Lyon

UNTIL ALEX'S CALL, BRUNO HAD slipped to the back of Eugene's mind. But now he came center stage. Perhaps he ought to try to reach him one more time before accepting the fact that Bruno would be of no further help in his quest to corner Jacques Mornnais.

Bruno answered immediately, "*Oui*," just as Jacques did.

"How are you, my friend, we haven't spoken in a while."

"I had a little run-in with some guys in Lyon, thought it might be better to go elsewhere, I'm in Marseille now."

"Oh really? Marseille?"

"Yeah, and you know who else is here? Your friend, the blonde, I pulled her out of the bushes a few days ago."

Eugene pretended surprise: "Pulled her out of the bushes? What was she doing there?"

"Some guy on a bike ran her off the path. Anyway, I have some other news. I found that bitch Caroline, the one that got my sister into all that trouble."

"You did what?"

"Do you remember the house on Traverse Paul, the one that you went to?" Eugene recalled his visit to the house. He'd been looking for Nicolas Pagès' records. He hadn't found any files, but some scraps of paper in a garbage bag had led to Caroline Trabert's name on a list of passengers headed to Thailand.

Bruno continued, "I went to take a last look for the art dealer's records. I couldn't go in because guess who was there: the kid I roughed up, his mother and some girl. They were arguing about money."

"You found Caroline Trabert?"

"Yeah. The guy who sent me over said only go into the house if it's empty. But that was then. Now, I'm going to finish the job."

"Slow down, Bruno. What do you mean, 'Finish the job?'"

"I mean that I'm going to get my sister's share of the money. And I need your help."

Eugene remembered seeing Patrick after Bruno did what he called 'roughing him up a little.' Maybe if he were present, he could prevent Bruno from giving full vent to his anger. And he hadn't forgotten that Bruno might still be useful to him.

"By the way, who did you say the guy was that sent you over there?"

"I didn't say, but since you ask, his name is Sauveur Paoli, he's a lawyer here in Marseille that I'm working for."

"Why do you suppose Sauveur Paoli asked you to look for records in that house? Strange how it keeps popping up, don't you think?"

"Yeah, strange."

Eugene wondered if Bruno wasn't holding back on him. But maybe some thoughts remained deep in his mind, stifled.

"Anyhow, where are you, can you come here soon?"

Eugene said he'd drive down tomorrow morning. They agreed to meet for lunch in the Panier. They'd take care of business in the afternoon, and Eugene would drive on to La Clusaz to ski, as planned.

CHAPTER THIRTY-ONE

CHÂTEAU D'HÉLÈNE SAT ON A small hill at the end of a long tree-lined drive. Three low steps led to the entrance. At ground level, a line of windows near the top of the basement faced the drive. As the hill sloped downward behind the house, a portion of the basement's back wall was exposed. Inside the château, it was possible to enter the basement by descending a stairway from the entrance hall. There had been a door in the rear wall as well, but it had been bricked up many years ago. In some places, the material binding the stones had eroded over time. The cracks had been filled with cement, giving the wall the aspect of an ugly stone patchwork, in contrast to the château's elegant façade. No one of any significance was likely to pass by the rear wall, and none of the owners had paid much attention to it. Jacques, however, had made a change—not cosmetic but structural: a new rear doorway now provided a way into the basement.

The workmen had finished their job a few days ago, and Jacques could now contemplate his pool undisturbed. After finishing breakfast, he walked down the stone steps to the basement, and continued along the corridor that led to the pool. Jacques approached the glass-enclosed space, and his nostrils twitched as he sniffed, trying to see if he could smell the humid, chlorine infused air. But, as promised, the moist, humid air remained behind the glass panels, just like at Renaud Schneider's gallery.

Jacques opened the door and stepped inside, sat down on one of the *chaises longues* that were scattered around the pool, amidst potted palm trees. The pool shimmered in the light of the overhead lamps, and for a moment he felt quite foolish, sitting beside a swimming pool dressed in a suit and tie. It had not occurred to Jacques that he could take advantage of this new addition to his home and dip his toes in the water, perhaps swim a few lengths before he dropped exhausted on one of the chairs. If Bruno had been here, he would already be doing laps. He scolded himself as he pushed Bruno to the back of his mind.

Jacques walked to the small room at the back of the pool. Here was the brain that controlled the humidity, sanitation, and water level. At the push of a button, he could even make waves and create a current, although it was doubtful that he would. He ran his hand over the smooth metal surface of the door at the back of the control room. On the other side were weeds and brambles, but in their place, he imagined the covered entrance to the Schneider gallery.

Jacques left the pool and went back up the stairs. He felt the weight of the emptiness of the big house. Mila, Tarek, and Bruno, all were gone. He couldn't say that he missed any of them—it was just that they had helped to fill the space.

As Jacques paced from one reception room to another, his mind, following his feet, bounced from one thought to the next. There was a large, flat-screen television in one of the rooms. He thought it ugly, but it was better than installing the home cinema that Mila had wanted. He didn't enjoy watching movies—the missteps and foibles of those in the real world were so much more compelling. No, the television was only good for following the news, and he turned it on, the sound of the presenter's voice filling the void. Jacques paid no attention to the low noise until he glanced at the screen and saw the banner in red: "Coup d'état in Brezikstan."

He turned up the volume, but the journalist had already moved on to other events, only the chyron remained at the bottom of the screen. If the ousted rulers of Brezikstan had followed his investment advice, then they had nothing to worry about, assuming they could get out of the country alive.

Well, that was their problem, not his. His lips formed a thin smile. The new rulers of Brezikstan—of course, he knew who they were—would be calling him. For he had not only his network in France for selling their uranium, but he knew where so many of the bodies were buried as well.

The journalist had started to talk about the Wikileaks revelations. Jacques took a deep breath, and a weak smile froze on his face as he contemplated the new possibilities offered by the digital age. How much easier it was now to access secrets and indiscretions. There was a member of the National Assembly who hadn't paid any income tax for years. Or a junior minister whose collection of antique watches was worth many times his annual salary. And that senator who paid a nominal rent for a six-bedroom flat owned by the city of Paris. Jacques was skilled at using information, for leverage, or for embarrassment, as the situation required. And given his modest origins, he took pleasure in watching the objects of his attention experience significant discomfort.

He called out to Mercie to bring him a glass of mango juice and turned off the television.

Jacques reached for a file on the corner of his desk and walked through the reception rooms. A musty smell hit his nostrils as he unlocked the door to the library. Inside, a layer of dust coated the bookcases and the intricate moldings; Mercie's job description didn't include cleaning the library.

The Bird of Paradise wallpaper was faded despite the heavy drapes being drawn. Rare first editions lined the shelves. They had been included in the purchase price of the château; Jacques had reasoned that one day they would add to the value of the place, give it an additional cachet. Otherwise, they were of no interest to him. A few minutes later, he left the library, locked the door behind him and returned to his office, empty-handed.

CHAPTER THIRTY-TWO

Traverse Paul

IN THE AFTERNOON, VÉRONIQUE RAN out to the supermarket up
the road. Not that she felt like going shopping, but she wanted to escape
the tension between Patrick and his mother. Caroline reminded her of an
ugly beetle, and Véronique wished that she would go away and crawl under
a rock.

#   #   #

Eugene and Bruno, driving slowly up Traverse Paul, saw Véronique's
car pull out of the driveway. Eugene recognized her: "It's the Pagès girl,
Nicolas' daughter." He continued further up the road, did a U-turn so that the
car was facing in the direction of Avenue Clot-Bey and parked on the narrow
shoulder. Bruno grunted okay, saying nothing more.

"Let me handle it," said Eugene "We'll get what we want without any
need for violence."

The patio outside the kitchen was protected from the wind; the sun
was warm enough for Patrick and Caroline to sit outside, drink coffee, and

96

argue. The two men walked across the lawn, "Hello kid," said Bruno as they approached.

Caroline stood up, "Who the hell are you, and what the hell are you doing here? Perhaps you didn't notice, but this is private property."

"It's all right, mom," croaked Patrick. But the expression on his face belied his words: what was Eugene Stokes doing with the man who had given him a beating?

Eugene stepped in front of Bruno, "You must be Madame Trabert. It's a pleasure to meet you. This gentleman is the brother of your colleague, Sandra Picardeau, I'm sure you remember her?"

Caroline's heavily tanned face took on a grayish pallor. Patrick stared blankly at the patio wall, as though imagining that he was back at his old job in the kitchen at Citadel Sushi. Some birds landed in a nearby tree, rustling the dry leaves, chirping. Caroline played with her coffee cup, trying to remain calm. A few seconds passed, and then Eugene's voice cut through the silence, as he continued to speak: "Your little stunt has caused a lot of pain to Madame Picardeau, and we think you need to make things right."

Véronique had returned from the supermarket. She entered the house through the side door, carrying her groceries into the kitchen. Seeing the two men, she stormed out of the kitchen: "What the fuck is going on? You again," she said, looking at Eugene.

"Hello, Mademoiselle Pagès, it's nice to see you as well. I was just telling Madame Trabert that she has made life difficult for her friend Sandra. Very thoughtless and very unkind."

Caroline had composed herself. "Okay," she said in a firm, defiant voice, "What do you want?"

"Since Madame Picardeau has been treated as though she was your partner, it's only right that you should treat her like one. Half of the money, Madame Trabert, now."

"I don't have the fucking money," she shrieked, pointing at Patrick, "Ask *him*." Patrick slumped lower in his chair; it was not Eugene, but Bruno, who occupied his field of vision.

"Yeah," Bruno snarled, "Why don't you tell us about the money?"

Eugene placed his hand on Bruno's arm, "Let's all stay calm, I'm sure we'll work this out, won't we Patrick? Why don't you do as your mother says, and tell us about the money?"

It was not certain who terrified Patrick more, Eugene with his quiet voice, or Bruno with his threat of violence.

"It's in an account in Jersey," he said. "I put the money there to protect my mother." He explained what he had done. He sneered at Bruno, "You never noticed the pendant with the account information when you beat me up—pretty dumb, I'd say."

But Bruno didn't rise to the bait: "That's okay, kid, we'll get the money now."

Véronique had been standing behind Patrick. She walked around the table to face him, "So that's what you were up to when we went to Saint-Malo—why didn't you tell me?"

"There wasn't any reason for you to know," he mumbled.

"You're such an asshole, Patrick."

"Let's not get side-tracked here," said Eugene. "You're going to transfer one million Euros to Sandra,"

"Don't do it, Patrick," hissed Caroline.

Bruno stood with his arms crossed, looked at Patrick, and said softly, "Oh, I think he will."

"Do you want him to beat the shit out of me again?" yelled Patrick.

"I don't think that will be necessary," said Eugene. He turned to Caroline: "Either we settle this right now, or we'll turn you over to the police. You won't be able to work on your suntan in prison, and I'm afraid that Patrick here would be held as an accomplice. Don't be too greedy, Madame, you risk losing everything: your money and your son."

He nodded to Patrick. "Go and get your computer. Bruno here will go with you, just to make sure you don't do anything stupid."

When Patrick returned with his computer, Bruno handed him a sheet of paper.

"Transfer the one million euros into this account."

"How do I know this is going to your sister?"

"You don't. You'll just have to trust me."

Patrick looked at Eugene. "It's okay," Eugene said, "Just do it. As for what's left, that's between you and your mother."

After several minutes, Bruno checked his telephone. "The money's there. Thanks, kid."

Caroline sat like a limp rag doll, her elbows on the table, her hands wrapped around her head. Patrick, too, sat still, all the energy drained out of him.

"Well, I guess that's it, then," concluded Véronique. Unlike the others, she was bright and cheerful: the beginning of the end had started. "I've got groceries to unpack and things to do, so if you'll excuse me, I'll just step into the kitchen and get on with my life. "

CHAPTER THIRTY-THREE

"BEFORE YOU GO, THERE'S JUST one last thing, Mademoiselle Pagès," said Bruno.

"Yes?"

The low menacing voice continued: "I think your father kept his files here, and I'd like to look around. Maybe you can tell me where they are, save me some time?"

Eugene, looking at Bruno, ignoring Véronique: "I think I can help you there, Bruno. Nicolas' files are either in storage not too far from here, or in Fontainebleau. Why are you asking?"

"Because Sauveur Paoli wants to know, that's why I'm asking."

"But why, Bruno? And who is Sauveur Paoli?"

"Sauveur is my boss. He has a client who wants to get his hands on his files, maybe you know him, a guy named Merv Peters. And Sauveur bought a painting from Jacques Mornnais, and Nicolas was involved in that as well."

"Merv Peters, not him again!"

Eugene turned to Véronique. "If you don't mind, we'd like to go to your storage locker and look around."

"And if I do mind?"

Eugene took a deep breath, sighed: "There's no cause for you to worry.

I'm not interested in your father's, um, activities, but in his partnership with Mr. Mornnais." He added: "As I recall, you brought Merv Peters' files back to Fountainebleau last October, but perhaps Nicolas kept records for Mr. Paoli's painting."

As they left the house, Bruno turned to Eugene, "Why did the girl move the files, what was she afraid of?"

"Merv Peters; he was trying to get his hands on her father's records."

"Lucky for me that he was. Otherwise, I never would have found Caroline Trabert."

#   #   #

The Spring-like weather had disappeared: a cold wind blew in dark clouds that masked the sun, turning the sky into a patchwork of gray. Véronique's cheerful mood had dissipated with the change in the weather, as they drove to the Shurgard site in Bonneveine. She entered her code, and they drove in and unlocked her unit. Eugene leafed through Nicolas's client files, but there was no record for Sauveur Paoli.

"Of course," said Eugene, "Sauveur was one of Jacques' clients, so the file must be back in Fontainebleau." *Shit,* he thought. *I'm going to have to put off skiing for another day or two.* He looked at Bruno and then at Véronique: "We'll have to make a quick trip to Fontainebleau to find those records."

It looked to Véronique as if the beginning of the end might have to wait.

#   #   #

Fontainebleau

The house was cold. And Véronique wasn't much of a housekeeper: clothes were strewn over the backs of chairs, empty bottles were lined up against a wall in the kitchen. There was a pile of unwashed dishes in the sink that they hadn't bothered to load into the dishwasher. As soon as he stepped

101

inside the house, Eugene wanted to leave.

"Are the files still in the restaurant's basement?" he asked.

"I guess so," replied Patrick.

"Where's that?" asked Bruno.

"Asia Garden, it's just up the street."

Bruno felt a gnawing in the pit of his stomach—the hunger was making him edgy.

"Yeah, let's get something to eat while we're at it."

After they had eaten, Sum, who was the owner along with his wife, took them down to the cellar. The boxes with Nicolas Pagès's records were lined up against one of the rough stone walls. A harsh light shone from the fluorescent tube, buzzing softly.

"Let's get on with it," said Eugene. He intended to make one last stab at probing Bruno's mind for any nuggets related to Jacques Mornnais. And the sooner they finished looking through the files, the sooner he'd be able to turn his attention to Bruno.

As Eugene and Bruno sifted through the files, it was Bruno who laid his hands on the folder with Sauveur Paoli's name on it.

"Do you mind if I keep this," he asked. "I'd like to show it to Sauveur."

"No problem. Just let me look at it first." The file showed, as Eugene had surmised, that Jacques had sold the Signac directly to Sauveur; Nicolas had merely provided the provenance paperwork.

"Hold on a minute." Bruno had come across the file labeled 'B. Edremal.' Looking at the folder reminded him that he had lost *Storm Over the Sea*. *"Merde,"* he muttered, as he showed the file to Eugene.

"I'd like to keep this one," said Eugene, "it may come in handy at some point, you never know."

Bruno shrugged. "Yeah, whatever."

They closed the boxes, put them back in place. They had found what they had come for.

\#   \#   \#

They headed back to Véronique's house; Eugene and Bruno walking

102

some distance behind the couple.

"I was wondering, has our friend Jacques been on your mind?"

"Not really, except that he sent some goons to try to kill me when I was in Lyon. But that didn't work out."

"Well, now that you're living in Marseille…"

"Yeah, it gives me time to make plans."

"What kind of plans, Bruno? Do they by any chance include Jacques?"

"Sorry Eugene, but I don't want to talk about Jacques. All I can say is that now that my memories are returning there are things I need to finish up. But don't worry about me, I can take care of myself."

"I do worry that you'll do something rash, something that you'll regret later."

Bruno shrugged, "Whatever." They had reached the house; Eugene got into his car and watched Bruno speed off on his motorcycle. He suspected that Bruno's plans included Jacques Mornnais and he resolved to meet with Jacques before Bruno got to him.

CHAPTER THIRTY-FOUR

Marseille

A SLIVER OF LIGHT LEAKED under the door to the darkened room. Bruno, in bed but wide awake, held his arms stiffly at his sides, his fists clenched. He heard the noise his breath made as it whistled through his nose in short, shallow bursts. A shadow slipped soundlessly into the room, glided across the cold tile floor, and stood over him. *"On a bien dormi, mon petit?"* He squeezed his eyes shut and felt the shadow's presence in his bed. He sensed that he knew who the shadow was, but when Bruno opened his eyes, he could see only a blank where the face should have been. As he stared at the featureless face, the sound of a seagull screeching pierced the silence. Bruno woke up, drenched in sweat.

The seagull flew from Rue Breteuil to Rue Saint-Jacques, where it hovered until it saw the uncovered refuse bin. It squawked, landed swiftly yet lightly, and began to peck at an open bag of kitchen scraps. Sauveur stood across the street, watching the bird attack the garbage. *Loud and aggressive, a true denizen of Marseille.* It brought to his mind the Frioul archipelago, where hundreds of the birds made their home. He would have to take Charlotte there, even if the mating season was not until later in the spring.

It was mid-morning when Bruno arrived at Sauveur's office. The feeling of unease had stayed with him as he slid a thin folder across Sauveur's desk, "I think this is what you're looking for."

Bruno sat with his hands on his knees, staring out the window, while Sauveur leafed through the file. "There's not much here, is there? And how did you get this?"

"It's a long story, but don't worry, nothing illegal. If you want to know, your file was in a box in the basement of a Chinese restaurant in Fontainebleau. Nicolas Pagès's daughter put some of his records there for safekeeping. There are others stored out at Shurgard in Bonneveine. It seems that she got scared that someone was trying to steal the files—like a lawyer in Paris named Merv Peters. A familiar name, isn't it?"

Sauveur ignored Bruno's question: "I need to find out more about this trust in Switzerland that was supposed to be the owner of my painting."

Bruno shook his head, "By all means, but I think you'll find that that trust is a dead end. Your painting is either stolen, or it's a fake. That's how Jacques operates."

"Then why didn't you tell me sooner?" Sauveur snapped.

"I couldn't tell you any sooner—it was only a month ago that you mentioned that you had bought a painting from him last summer. And don't forget: I stopped working for Jacques last January."

#   #   #

Gregory Tomasso straightened his tie, put on his jacket, and with a feeling of apprehension, knocked on the door to Sauveur's office. He didn't relish being the bearer of bad news, and he hoped the boss would not take his anger out on him.

"Come in."

"Sir…I looked into the matter as you requested…"

"And, come out with it."

"Well, I found the accounts of a Marcus Leiberfeld Trust—the trust mentioned in the provenance document. The trust was liquidated in the 1990s. There was no mention of a painting in the assets that were distributed

105

to the beneficiaries. And, as far as I could tell, the trustees never bought or sold any paintings.

"So, we can conclude that my painting never belonged to the trust?"

"It looks like that, sir."

"I see. Thank you, Gregory. Well done."

At first, Sauveur was angry with himself. How could he have been so stupid, so thoughtless, and so gullible? He had to hand it to Jacques: he could be very compelling in his understated way. And the same was true for his expert, Nicolas Pagès. Jacques had seen his desire to flaunt his success and his wealth—wasn't everyone in Marseille a bit of a show-off—and had suckered him out of ten million dollars. The rage within solidified and morphed into anger at Jacques.

CHAPTER THIRTY-FIVE

Marseille

THE MESSAGE FROM *MAÎTRE* PAOLI was cryptic: he had news about the property that Merv had expressed an interest in. Could he come down to Marseille?

Merv and Sauveur had never met. They were a study in contrasts: the pale-skinned portly Paris lawyer and the olive-skinned silver fox from Marseille. Merv leaned forward, cracked his knuckles. He had the habit of drawing his lips tightly across his gums to hide his snaggle-toothed smile. Sauveur looked at him intently.

"You remind me of someone I knew a long time ago in Paris, but his name was Ralph, not Merv. "

"My full name is Mervin Ralph Peters, have we met before?" As he asked the question, he continued, "You're Sasha, aren't you?"

Sauveur leaned back and laughed. "What an incredible coincidence. You were the American who hung around with us on Rue des Trois Frères, aren't you? "

"The same, only with more pounds, I'm afraid."

"And do you remember a girl named Charlotte? It turns out that she's spending the winter in Marseille!"

"Charlotte? No, I don't think that I do."

"It's too bad you're not staying longer, she's in Paris right now, but she'll be back in January. We could have met for a drink, for old time's sake."

"Yes, that is unfortunate, but I'll be long gone." He went on, without stopping: "So, I think you have some news for me?"

"Yes, the good news is that we've located the records that Nicolas Pagès kept that mention your transactions. Getting your hands on them will be complicated, but we could try to do it."

"Of course, I want to do it!"

"But why, my friend?"

"Because I want to sell my collection, turn the page and move back to the States."

"It was Jacques Mornnais who helped you to assemble your collection, is that right?"

"Yes, that's right."

"Well, my friend, I'm sorry to tell you that chances are good that all of your paintings are either fakes or stolen."

"Why do you say that? Nicolas Pagès certified the authenticity of all my paintings. I'm sure the supporting documents are in those records you mentioned."

"Ralph—may I call you Ralph—I have learned from a man who used to work for Jacques Mornnais that he dealt in fakes and stolen goods."

"Who is this man?"

"A fellow named Bruno Edremal. I think you know him?"

Merv nodded, yes, he knew the man.

Sauveur continued, "But let me ask you something: you bought many paintings through Monsieur Mornnais; did you never suspect anything?"

Merv sighed. "Only when he said he had no records of the provenance."

"I see. If it's any consolation, Jacques Mornnais has cost me a great deal of money. And I don't know about you, but I intend to get my money back."

Sauveur watched as Merv shook his head, ran his hands through his hair, cracked his knuckles. It was always interesting to see how people reacted to bad news.

Merv leaned forward, placed his hands on the edge of Sauveur's desk: "Yes, I intend to get my money back as well."

\#   \#   \#

The two men parted company. Sauveur hadn't bothered to ask Merv why he had not joined them in their late-night prank so many years ago. He was sure he knew the answer: Merv was one of those people who like to pretend to be someone—a revolutionary, an art collector, a man about town—they were not. He'd probably bragged to his friends back home that he'd been part of their little caper. Thirty years later, he was the same: older, fatter but still the same knuckle-cracking, snaggle-toothed loser.

\#   \#   \#

Merv hadn't thought about Charlotte in years, but now her face peeked out from the folds of his memory. It had felt so good to sleep with the woman who had been Sasha's girlfriend. It sounded like Charlotte had not mentioned that to Sauveur. In fact, he need not have worried, for he had slipped from Charlotte's memory as soon as he had left her apartment for the last time.

CHAPTER THIRTY-SIX

Château d'Hélène

EARLY MORNING. IN THE SOUNDLESS darkness, Jacques was packing his suitcase. As the sun rose, he saw that the fog had rolled in overnight. It wrapped a pale grey-white blanket around the château, little gauzy bits stretched over the shrubs and hung over the frozen ground. The fog was like a gossamer-thin wall. It threatened to slow them down and they would have to leave for the airport earlier than planned.

He was closing his suitcase when the phone rang. "Paoli" flashed on the screen. He knew he couldn't continue to avoid Sauveur: "*Oui?*" he answered.

"Hello Jacques, you're not an easy man to reach."

"Yes."

"There's a problem with the painting you sold me—the Signac, I'm sure you remember. It looks like it's a fake, so we need to do something about that."

"I'm surprised to hear that; it came with an impeccable provenance."

"Jacques, please, let's cut the bullshit. The provenance is anything but impeccable. It's a load of crap, and I want my money back."

"I'm leaving for Asia this morning. Let's meet when I get back. I'm sure there has been some mistake."

"The only mistake was my trusting you. I expect my money back by mid-January. Otherwise, I'll let everyone know how dishonest you are."

"It's not necessary to threaten me Sauveur, we'll sort this out on my return, I promise you."

Jacques sat on the edge of his bed, waited for his hands to stop trembling. He couldn't put off Sauveur Paoli as easily as Merv Peters. Outside, the fog had started to dissipate, but the trip to the airport would still take longer than usual, giving him plenty of time to make a few phone calls. Lawyers were such a pain; he'd have to remember to avoid dealing with them in the future.

#   #   #

Sauveur, too, trembled, but with rage. Jacques had made minimal effort to convince him that his painting was genuine, as if he didn't really care that the Signac was a fake. Jacques had dismissed his complaint as though it was of minor importance: how infuriating. If Sauveur was no stranger to cutting corners, for him, there was a difference between stretching the law and breaking it. And, if Jacques thought that once he'd paid him off, Sauveur would keep his little racket to himself, he was sadly mistaken.

Sauveur looked at his watch and realized he needed to leave for a meeting at the town hall. He left his office, walked down Rue Saint-Jacques, and turned onto Rue Breteuil. Three buildings had been demolished, gouging out an empty space, surrounded by a high wooden fence. He smiled as he thought of the battle to get the authorization to replace those old edifices by a sleek, modern structure. They had found apartments for the tenants who had been forced to leave. Perhaps their new residences were not in the center of the city—real estate values were too high—but at least they were not homeless. The only problem had been the rats; the construction had disturbed them, forced them to flee their habitat. They had scaled outdoor pipes looking for a new place to live, causing residents in the nearby buildings to complain. *Always something*, he thought, but not surprising, though: there were more rats than people in Marseille. As he slowed down to take a closer look at the building site, a black form emerged from behind the wooden fence, the sun glinting off its sleek coat. Sauveur watched as the rat stopped to pick up an apple core in the gutter. Its tiny pink paws looked so human to him. He stared after the rat as it scurried away. It reminded him of another fat rat, this one two-legged.

CHAPTER THIRTY-SEVEN

Lyon

IN THE PAST, AT THE start of the Christmas holiday, Bruno would fly to Singapore with Jacques and Mila. After he left them, he would go on to Thailand and indulge his preference for younger women. But since his accident, his libido had disappeared along with his taste for alcohol.

This year, he would not be heading for sun-drenched beaches and warm *café au lait* bodies. Instead, he walked through Gare Saint-Charles, under lights strung up for the holiday, and waited for the announcement of the departure for Lyon. He stood to the rear of the crowd. And reflected on how easy it would be to relieve some of the travelers of their wallets. One woman caught his attention. She paced nervously back and forth, continually lifting her eyes to read the notice board as if willing the track letter to appear. She was so preoccupied that he thought it would be fun to lift something out of her backpack, but—a rueful smile crossed his lips—he was no longer in that line of work.

The letter "J" flashed on the screen, and a ripple passed through the crowd as the travelers hurried to catch the train. He stepped aside to let them pass. There was no point in rushing; the train would not leave for another twenty minutes. The woman he had noticed earlier hurried past him. He realized with a start that it was Caroline Trabert, the kid's mother. He followed her as she walked down the platform of track J. So, they were taking the same train. When he saw that the train's destination was Brussels, he guessed that Caroline would be taking a flight back to Thailand. Bruno almost felt sorry for her—a skinny older woman with a rucksack bouncing on her back as she dragged her suitcase along the platform. Had she gotten her money back from her son, he wondered. Well, it wasn't his problem, and he didn't need to know.

The train was packed, every seat taken. A baby cried intermittently, couples discussed their holiday plans, cell phones rang. Less than two hours later, the train arrived in Lyon. One group of travelers left the train, another small crowd waited to board. As he made his way slowly towards the exit, he turned his head towards the waiting train. Caroline was in a window seat, staring at him. He waved and walked down the ramp.

Gare Part-Dieu was thick with people: commuters, students, holidaymakers. It should have been slow going, yet Bruno progressed through the crowd unimpeded. He was a big man, but it was not his size alone that caused people to move out of his way. Instead, something about him was frightening, like an evil aura that pulsed out from his body.

Once outside the station he took a taxi to Sandra's apartment. He remembered arriving in Lyon last January, with no memory and no money. How different things were now. He still had a few loose ends to tie up; he would start with Sandra and then move on to his other business.

#   #   #

Bruno had the taxi drop him at Place des Terreaux and climbed up Montée de la Grande Côte until he reached n°102. Sandra was still at work, and he let himself into the apartment. Bruno had left Lyon less than two months ago, yet it seemed much longer than that. In the refrigerator, he found an open bottle of Badoit. It tasted a little flat, but he was thirsty and gulped it down. He unpacked his suitcase, then took the free newspaper he had been reading and sat in the easy chair in the living room and waited for Sandra to come home.

She was surprised to see him there; Bruno had left a message that he would be coming to Lyon for the holidays, but he hadn't said exactly when he'd arrive. How was he, she asked, what was he doing? He told her a little about Sauveur, enough to satisfy her curiosity.

"And how are you doing," he asked.

"Oh, you know, the same, I guess. "

"I have some good news for you."

"Yes?"

"I found your friend Caroline, it was an accident, but I found her. And then with a pal, we persuaded her to share the money that she stole."

Sandra sat very still. She had wanted to hear those words—or ones with that meaning—for months, but there was something about Bruno that was a bit off, and she couldn't help but ask, "How did you do that? Nothing violent, I hope."

"Not to worry. It was the American—you remember meeting him here last summer, don't you—who helped me. And he's a regular Boy Scout."

Bruno went into the kitchen to find another bottle of water. "Do you want some Badoit?" he called to Sandra.

"No thanks, I'm OK."

Back in the living room, he continued: "The money is in an offshore account I opened years ago. We need to open an account for you where I can transfer the money. But then you'll have to be very careful about where and how you spend it."

Sandra blinked rapidly; otherwise, she was still. Did Bruno expect her to smile, to say how happy she was, to thank him for what he had done?

When she said nothing, he asked, "What's the matter, I thought you'd be jumping for joy?"

She breathed deeply, then smiled: "Thank you, dear Bruno. I'm just so surprised. Frankly, I never expected this."

Indeed, Sandra had grown accustomed to being hurt and angry: she wore her feelings like a well-cut, close-fitting coat. The cause of her outrage had disappeared, and she felt suddenly naked and empty.

"I've been angry for so long, it's going to take some time for me to let go. But I will!"

"Well, you need to think about things. There's no rush, we can talk some more when you're ready."

CHAPTER THIRTY-EIGHT

BRIGHTLY COLORED LIGHTS WERE STRUNG around the square in front of Chez Michel, twinkling in the foggy sky. Bruno had worked in the little restaurant after he had returned to Lyon last January. It was here that he'd come across Alex and Marie-Agnès, it was here that he'd met Eugene Spector, the man who had helped him to retrieve some of his memories. He'd felt restless after talking with Sandra, let down that she wasn't more excited that he'd found Caroline and recovered the money that she'd nagged him about incessantly. It was funny how she found it difficult to let go of unpleasant thoughts, thoughts that had become a part of her being. But then again, in trying to figure out what his dark dreams meant, wasn't he doing the same thing?

Michel looked up from behind the bar, felt Bruno's presence before he walked through the door.

"*Salut*, you're back in Lyon?"

"Not really, just visiting my sister for the holidays. Then I'll be off again."

Michel didn't bother to ask Bruno where he'd be off to; if he wanted him to know, he would have told him. As far as he was concerned, Bruno had done a good job, didn't drink, didn't steal from the till, and the rest was not his problem.

"Something to drink?"

"An espresso, thanks."

Michel slid the small china cup and saucer across the counter: "About a week after you were gone, some guy came by, asked if you were around. He ordered a drink, tried to get me to talk about you. I had nothing to tell him and said so. Then he left. End of the story."

Michel wiped the counter's dull silver surface: "Oh yeah, I don't think he was French, he had some kind of foreign accent."

Bruno gazed at the bottles lined up on glass shelves against the wall: "Do you remember what he looked like?"

"He was a big guy, like you. Fair-haired. I didn't really pay much attention."

Bruno had finished his coffee and reached into his pocket for change. Michel told him not to bother, and he hoped Bruno would stop by again.

#   #   #

Bruno walked to the Cour des Voraces and headed down to Old Town. He smirked as he remembered the two men Jacques had sent after him and the one who had come looking for him at Chez Michel. By now, Jacques must have known that he was working for Sauveur, he'd have to be careful when he was back in Marseille. But today, he had other things on his mind.

Looming over Place Saint-Jean was the Lyon Cathedral, a medieval architectural masterpiece built over the space of several hundred years and completed in the fifteenth century. He checked his watch—it was ten minutes to four: he was on time. Had the weather been more clement, a crowd would have been gathered inside in front of the world-famous astronomical clock. But the cathedral was almost deserted, for the damp cold weather had frightened away all but the hardiest tourists.

As he approached the clock, he saw a group of young boys, perhaps eight or nine years old, accompanied by a figure in a long black robe—he must have been a priest. He heard the man explain to the children that the clock was one of the oldest in Europe. "Take a close look at the astrolabe.

Do you see the date, the position of the moon, the sun, and the earth? And do you see the stars in the sky over Lyon? But remember, this clock was built in the Middle Ages, so you'll see that the sun is shown circling the earth. Now, watch and listen!" The clock struck four o'clock, a rooster crowed three times, and animated figures—angels and a dove—moved. Bruno closed his eyes to shut out the noise. When he opened them, all was quiet again. The priest and the boys had disappeared.

His armpits were wet, his neck damp: despite the cold, he was sweating. Bruno strode quickly out of the cathedral, his hands jammed into the pockets of his jacket to keep them from shaking. It was on a class trip to visit the cathedral that he had seen the priest for the first time. He stopped at the entrance to the Fourvière funicular; *do I really want to go on with this?* And bought his ticket.

Some minutes later, the funicular arrived at the Fourvière Basilica station. Bruno crossed the street and entered the church. He had never liked the building; he thought that the exterior, with its four towers, was graceless and ugly. And inside, the walls, carpeted with mosaics, reminded him of an expensive Moroccan restaurant. His mother had brought him and Sandra to attend Mass here, and the only memory that surfaced was the feeling of boredom. He was disappointed; somehow, he had expected something more, a clue to unlocking the mystery of his black dreams.

He entered the park next to the church, and gazed at the city of Lyon, spread out below. The sun had now set, and a thousand lights twinkled in the darkness. He picked out monuments, made out the Saone and the Rhône, circling the *Presqu'ile* where Sandra lived. But he felt nothing, saw no wisps of images, had no fleeting thoughts. Nothing. Perhaps a walk down to the river Saone would bring his hidden memories out into the open.

Bruno started to walk along Montée de l'Observance, a long street that led to the right bank of the Saone. He had walked perhaps 100 meters when he stopped outside a two-story house. It was set back from the street, behind a garden that was a graveyard of shriveled branches, dead plants, and patches of dried grass. A dim yellow light filtered from behind the drapes on the ground floor. The upper story was dark. On a ceramic plaque set into the gate, he read *Centre d'études Saint-Bernard.* He put his hands on his head to

119

stop the pounding in his temples that shut out all noise from the street. The front door opened, a black-clad figure stepped out, threw a bag of garbage into a brown plastic bin, and retreated quickly into the warmth of the house. A cold wind blew up from the river, pushing Bruno to continue walking down the street. The house was not familiar, and yet he knew that he would return to have a closer look.

CHAPTER THIRTY-NINE

Fresh Meadows, New York

THE CHRISTMAS PARTIES HAD STARTED at the beginning of December. Merv was a fixture in both the French and Anglo-American legal communities, and his dance card quickly filled up with cocktails and dinners. Jacques had always organized a party in the cellars of the *Maison de Nature et de la Chasse*—it was an event where you went to see and to be seen. But this year, Merv had not received the customary engraved invitation, and neither had any of his acquaintances. Merv awoke on the twentieth of December and realized that everyone who counted was either away in the sun, or skiing or at a country home.

At loose ends, he called his sister and announced that he would be arriving in Fresh Meadows on the twenty-second. It hadn't occurred to him to ask if she had any plans for the holidays. Since he was the one with money, he assumed that she would make the necessary adjustments to her holiday plans.

His sister Phyllis, a grammar school teacher, had indeed plans of her own. But since she was unable to assert herself to anyone over the age of eight, she put everything on hold pending her brother's arrival.

He grabbed a taxi at the airport. They drove to Fresh Meadows, a sprawling, middle-class property development where he and his sister had grown up. He did not visit often, and when he did, he compared his early life in the borough of Queens with his current status. Merv rubbed shoulders with the good and the great, maybe he had to suck up to some of them but still, he had come a long way.

At the entrance to Fresh Meadows, they drove past a huge Christmas tree, decorated with red and white globes. The lawns in front of the garden apartments were crowded with elves and sleighs, giant candy canes and reindeer. Santa Clauses with one leg up, hung outside windows, or were perched on rooftops. Lights outlined some of the houses or were strung up around the bare trees and shrubs, and he thought he heard Christmas music emanating from one of the lawns. He was thoroughly depressed by the time the taxi stopped in front of the apartment block where Phyllis lived.

"Mervin," she stretched out her arms to greet him. Phyllis' short dark hair, laced with gray, was cropped close to her head; she could have passed for a little man.

If Phyllis was wired to avoid confrontation, that didn't mean that she was condemned to silence. She observed Merv as he slumped into her rocking chair: the bags under his blood-shot eyes, his skin's grayish pallor, and his disheveled hair. He looked like hell.

"You look like you could use a drink," she told him and brought him a scotch on the rocks, Johnny Walker Black Label that he had brought over when he visited in September.

"I was surprised when you called. You haven't been back to visit in years, and now, two visits in four months. Is everything OK?"

"Yeah, fine. I just thought that it'd be nice to spend the holidays together, we haven't done that in a long time."

"Oh yes, of course, I see," she said, although she didn't see at all.

#   #   #

Phyllis didn't have to change her plans. As Merv had none of his own, he tagged along as she met with friends and colleagues. *These people are so fucking boring, what am I doing with these losers?* His feeling of self-pity blossomed: red and angry, like a case of adolescent acne. Why hadn't he stayed in France, he asked himself, he had a lovely home at Saint-Germer-de-Fly. Instead, he was surrounded by a bunch of spinster schoolteachers in an insurance company development; he was glad his friends could not see him here.

"How exciting to live in Paris - what do you do there?"

He realized that someone was talking to him. A black straw hat sat atop a cloud of thin dark gray hair. Layers of clothing covered her massive frame: his eyes moved downwards from a shirt, a vest, and a short-sleeved jacket, to a skirt with flounces. Perhaps there were more garments in the monochromatic mountain of white, gray, and black, he couldn't be sure.

The nose was too big, and the lips were too thin. But she had lively, intelligent eyes. In any event, Merv had to respond: "Yes, it is quite exciting. I have a law practice where I deal mostly with ex-pats. And," he could not resist adding, "I'm an art collector."

"How interesting! I have a small art gallery right here in Fresh Meadows. Perhaps you'd like to visit?"

Merv had a vision of the cheesy paintings he'd seen at all too many art shows: garish abstracts, boring landscapes, dull still lifes. "Uh, thanks, I'd love to, but I'm kind of short on time; I'm only here for a few days."

Phyllis cut in: "Sylvia, if we can, we will, I promise."

After they left, as they walked home, Phyllis asked Merv why he didn't want to visit Sylvia's gallery. He stopped and sighed: "First of all because I know the kind of shit that one finds in those little galleries, and second because I'm trying to sell my collection, not add to it."

"Well, maybe she could help you, who knows?"

"Highly unlikely." He was wondering whether to tell his sister that he had doubts about his paintings when he became aware of *"Rudolph the Red-Nosed Reindeer"* blaring from the lawn in front of them. Rudolph and his fellow reindeer were pulling a sleigh, a red light flashing on his nose.

"I hate this holiday shit," he hissed. "Sorry, Phyllis, but I guess Christmas is not my thing." He tried to wipe Rudolph from his mind and, at the same time, decided that she didn't need to know that he had a collection of fakes and stolen property. Challenging as it was, he would try to enjoy his time in Fresh Meadows.

CHAPTER FORTY

ON FRIDAY, DECEMBER 24TH, EUGENE sped down a black slope at
La Clusaz. He was a natural skier and had he grown up in the mountains
instead of the suburbs of Virginia, he might have skied competitively. As it
was, Eugene enjoyed the feeling of freedom, his skis flying over the snow,
the wind stinging his lips. He was present in this moment; there was no
other. Years ago, Eugene had a ski instructor who told him that he had great
potential. So many people had said to him that he had great potential for so
many things. Yet he found himself in the French Alps wondering just what
he had achieved.

He thought about the recent series of fortuitous circumstances that
resulted in Bruno's recovering his sister's share of the funds that Caroline
Trabert had embezzled. But any illusions he'd had that Bruno would be
grateful for his help—or that he'd cough up any useful memories about
Jacques Mornnais' activities—had been shattered outside the house
in Fontainebleau.

A few days ago, Pascal Navarro had called to ask about Eugene's
progress on the special project he had outlined when they had last met. *The
nerve of the guy, calling me right before Christmas. Doesn't he ever take
time off?* Eugene remembered sharing a beer with Travis last October. His

friend had warned him to stay away from Jacques Mornnais. But Eugene had promised Pascal that he'd do his best to get the compromising files Jacques kept on France's political and business elite. He needed to stop procrastinating and get ready to confront Jacques in the New Year. The more he thought about it, the more he was confident that he'd be able to use Thomas Smith's notes to achieve the desired result.

Outside, the trees were heavy with newly fallen snow—it was a picture-postcard view. He pushed Bruno and Jacques to the back of his mind, determined not to let the unholy couple's image mar the enjoyment of his ski holiday.

Alex's image had taken their place. He wanted—he needed— to talk to her, but it was Christmas Eve, he was sure she was busy with her family.

#   #   #

Neuilly-sur-Seine

Every year, members of the Vesla de Trubenne clan gathered on Christmas Eve and again on Christmas day. When Chloe was alive, she and Richard had preferred to spend the holiday season in Seychelles. Richard found the holiday celebrations boring, but as Alex had expressed a desire to meet her cousins, he invited some of the family to spend Christmas Eve at his home.

Charlotte had warned her that the cousins—bankers, lawyers, and senior civil servants—were stuffy and given to monotonous conversation. She had not been mistaken, but Alex tried to show interest in the stories they told about people she had never met. The cousins enquired about Richard's health—he was feeling fine, thank you—and asked about the work being done at Trubenne. They resented Richard for having bought their parents out but refrained from mentioning it. And Alex suspected that they resented her and Charlotte as well, for the three of them were the sole shareholders in the Trubenne property. When one shareholder died, the survivors would inherit their shares. In all probability, Alex would one day be the sole owner of Trubenne.

"You'll have to come down and visit us next summer," said Richard, although it was doubtful that he'd be going forward with that invitation.

The evening started with the exchange of gifts. Alex had been assigned cousin Vital, a taciturn lawyer with a cold smile. Richard told her that Vital was a wine connoisseur, so she had trudged over to Lavinia, a wine supermarket near the Madeleine, and bought a magnum of Saint-Emilion. Vital had offered her a pink china mug with a tea strainer.

As the dinner dragged on, Alex did her best to smile, laugh, and be pleasant, but it was an uphill battle. They had started with champagne, then Chablis to accompany an entrée of scallops and leeks, followed by a Château Margaux and roast leg of lamb. After the salad, cheese, and the obligatory *Bûche de Nöel,* she started to wonder if the evening would ever end. Now she understood Richard's reticence to organize a dinner with the cousins. Alex was grateful that her uncle had tried to please her, but this was an activity that need not be repeated.

The door closed as the last of the cousins headed out into the night. The silence in the apartment wrapped itself around Alex like an old, familiar quilt. She didn't feel like talking about the evening, excused herself, took a large Doliprane, and slipped into bed.

When Alex awoke on Christmas day, she was slightly hung-over, more than slightly depressed. She vowed that next year she would sit out the holiday season far from the forced gaiety of omnipresent Christmas music and rituals of gift giving. She took another Doliprane, made herself a cup of tea in her new pink mug, and melted into the sofa cushions. The mug made her think briefly of Vital, he reminded her of a giant black spider. Then Eugene, who had been lurking at the edges of her mind, came back onto center stage. *I must try not to think about him anymore, there's no point to it.*

The Doliprane and tea worked their magic: Alex got up, showered, and dressed. Richard and Charlotte had gone out for a walk, and she rummaged in the kitchen, making lunch from last night's leftovers. There was an open bottle of Château Margaux on the counter; her hangover gone, she poured herself a glass. The alcohol soothed her, softened the hard edges, and when Eugene called, there was no trace of hostility in her voice.

"Merry Christmas, Alex."

"Yes, Merry Christmas to you Eugene."

The banalities taken care of, he cut to the chase. "Look, Alex, "I know that I haven't behaved properly, but I've had a lot on my plate. I also know that's no excuse, and we need to talk. If you're not too busy with your family, I was thinking of coming up to Paris—I could be there the day after tomorrow. What do you think?"

"What about your ski holiday? And your friends?"

"Alex, listen to me. Seeing you is much more important than another run down the black slopes."

Alex was silent for a moment, taking it all in. She'd been imagining what she'd say to Eugene if only they could meet, and now he was proposing the very thing she'd dreamt of. And suddenly she was afraid of what he might say.

"That's okay," she started to reply. She was about to continue, "I'll be back in Marseille next week—let's get together then. I'll call you after Charlotte and I have returned," but stopped. *Better to get this over with once and for all.* "Yes, I'm free the day after tomorrow. Where would you like to meet?"

Eugene gave her the address of the hotel on Avenue de Wagram where he usually stayed. "That's great. Looking forward to it. Take care, Alex."

CHAPTER FORTY-ONE

EUGENE WAS WAITING FOR ALEX in the hotel's small lobby. She wore her blue pleated ensemble that matched her eyes (*I need to wear something that makes me feel good*). A quick chuckle as she put on the white parka she'd worn the day Bruno had pulled her out of the bushes.

The golden flecks danced in Eugene's eyes as he put his arms around Alex. "I'm so happy to see you," he whispered as he pulled her closer. She savored the moment. "How about going to our usual watering hole? The Café Carré is just a few blocks away."

On the way over, small talk about the crowds at La Clusaz—he wasn't going skiing at Christmas next year, just too many rude people to cope with. Travis and Julie's chalet and Julie's cooking. The *reveillon* at Richard's apartment, meeting the Vesla de Trubenne clan—quite the experience. And then they were at the doors of Café Carré.

They were seated, there was an awkward silence, neither sure how to begin. The waiter brought their order: an espresso for Alex and a beer for Eugene. Alex brought the cup to her lips, took a sip, and placed the cup back on the saucer, the clink sounding like a cue to begin.

"I'm glad you called and that you've come to see me. There's something I've wanted to ask you. What I mean is, everything seemed so great between us when we were at Trubenne, and then you turned so cold when we spoke on the phone after that. I guess I'm wondering what happened?"

Eugene had anticipated Alex asking that question. But now that she had, as he looked at her troubled face, the issue seemed so unimportant. Yet he knew that he owed her an explanation.

"Do you remember the painting 'Storm Over the Sea?' You know, the one where I got you a reward for the maid that found it? The one that I returned to the church? Quite by accident, I came across that very painting at Trubenne, hidden away with some junk. You never mentioned that there were two copies, and so naturally, I wondered why you hadn't said anything. Then too, I remembered the woman who sat outside the office I had rented. I didn't think much of it at the time, but now that I've met her, I have a hunch that would have been Marie-Agnès. Am I mistaken? So, I guess you could say that I was disappointed that you didn't seem to trust me…."

Alex could feel herself tearing up. She swallowed, took a sip of coffee, regained her composure. "You're right, I didn't trust you. I still don't, even though I wish that I could. But I've always felt that there are so many things that you don't tell me. Like where did that ten-thousand-dollar reward really come from? And why did you get the money for Ella? I was able to get in touch with Li, and he did a copy of the painting for me. Do you really think it makes any difference? I'm sure it's of no importance to the priest."

"Ah, Alex, you were around our Mr. Mornnais for too long. Of course, it makes a difference, even if the priest couldn't tell them apart."

"But you haven't answered my question: who are you and what are you really up to?"

Eugene sensed that he was losing Alex. "Well, if you must know, it's a long story."

For the first time, Alex smiled. "I've got nothing but time right now."

Eugene gestured to the waiter—"Another espresso?" he asked her. "No thanks, I'm OK."—and ordered a second beer. Silence. The gold flecks had faded as he swallowed, his eyes on Alex, yet far away. She sipped her coffee. It was cold, but she needed something to do with her hands while she waited for Eugene to collect his thoughts.

#   #   #

"Where to begin? I think I remember telling you about my Aunt Madeleine, the one who bequeathed the phony Poussin to my sister. Madeline had no children of her own, she doted on me and Kate, and when she passed away, my sister and I inherited her estate. By then, I had begun to feel dissatisfied with my work at the bureau—perhaps it was burnout or perhaps a realization that I didn't really fit in. My inheritance gave me the opportunity to take some time off from work, but I didn't want to burn my bridges completely, so I had to negotiate a leave of absence. The result was that I agreed to carry out a mission for the Bureau as a condition of getting my leave. There was a rumor that someone in France kept a file, not unlike J. Edgar Hoover: he had the information on the peccadillos of those in power—whether in government, industry, or the military. And he would use that information as leverage, for a price. My bosses were certain that person was Jacques Mornnais—and my mission was to get his files."

A faint touch of pink appeared on Alex's cheeks. "So, you've been focused on Jacques all this time," she said.

"Yes, he seems to be at the center of so much activity, he's a criminal polymath."

"Well, that was quite a coincidence running into me in Parc Monceau, or did it all start when you rented my house?"

Eugene shook his head, "No, renting your house was purely random. But when we saw the photos of you and Jacques entering one of those fancy restaurants, we couldn't pass up the opportunity to get closer to him through you."

"And paying the reward was a way to stay close to me."

"Yes, Alex, but by then, I wanted to be close to you, independent of my work."

"And the man in the blue anorak, he was working for you?"

"Yes, how do you know that?"

"I saw you walking with him on Champ de Mars, and then again in the café where I met you. And I recognized him when you and he came to Nathalie Martin's apartment after Tarek attacked us. Is he still working for you?"

"No, why do you ask?"

"Oh, just curious."

After a moment's silence, she said, "You may have the right to be annoyed that I switched the paintings, but I was right not to trust you."

He took her hands in his, "Alex, when this all started, I didn't know you, I had to be careful. And afterward, I didn't know how to explain everything. I hope it's not too late now to start over."

Alex smiled weakly. "I don't know, I have to get used to the idea." She smiled more broadly, lifted his hand to her lips, and kissed it.

To Eugene, it seemed like a new beginning, even if he had held back a few cards; he just couldn't help himself.

#   #   #

Alex felt like skipping like a schoolgirl as she walked back to Neuilly. Her thoughts mirrored Eugene's: could this be a new beginning? Maybe this time it *was* different. Eugene would be returning to La Clusaz for the remainder of the holiday, and Alex and Charlotte would be back in Marseille at the beginning of January. They agreed that she'd let him know as soon as they got back, and he'd come to visit them in Marseille. It seemed like a perfect start to the New Year.

CHAPTER FORTY-TWO
January 2011

Château d'Hélène

JACQUES DIDN'T CARE MUCH FOR the holidays. He was happiest—perhaps "fulfilled" would be more accurate—when he practiced the art of deception. Selling fake paintings to men like Merv and Sauveur excited him. It was quite an achievement for the son of Portuguese immigrants; it had taken only a single generation to make the leap from poverty to wealth.

He liked the surge of power he felt when dealing with the government of Brezikstan. It didn't matter which group of thugs was running the country. As long as he took care of paying commissions to the buyers, and the local tax—better known as bribes—to the sellers, all was well. Nothing had changed since the recent *coup d'Etat.* Jacques knew the new government, some had even been members of the old regime, and he knew many of their secrets, and that ensured that he was indispensable.

Yes, the holidays were at last over. Jacques had visited his lawyers in Singapore. He'd spent some time renewing old friendships—you never knew when these people could come in handy—and took a few days to go to Montenegro and check on the paintings he had shipped there last Spring. He had made the most of his time off. A man in his position didn't stay home for the holidays—but now he was excited to bring his latest project to fruition.

He had called his new Brezikstan friends and asked them to send some of their specialists to meet with him. Four men had driven to the château. It turned out that he had worked with all of them before—regimes might change, but the worker bees remained.

The plans for the Schneider Gallery's underground garage were spread out on a table in one of the reception rooms—a friend in the Paris Mayor's office had been happy to provide them. Against one wall was an open storage space for packing materials, and next to the storage space, there was a door. On the other side of the door was the control room to the Schneiders' swimming pool.

Jacques explained what he had in mind. The entire family would be leaving on a two-week ski vacation in January, before the start of the French school holidays. They thought nothing of closing the gallery for two weeks, which provided a perfect window of opportunity.

The team would drive their van into the courtyard and open the door to the basement. From there they would enter the gallery by the door to the swimming pool. He unfolded floor plans of the gallery; the objects to be taken were marked in red.

"You'll have to disable the alarm system," and he placed the system's plans on the table.

"Normally, only the Schneider family has access to the garage, but you'll have to be sure that the door to the street cannot be opened while you're in the gallery. "

The leader, a short, wiry man, in his 40's, his head shaved clean, nodded: "Yes," he said in heavily accented English, "We've done this before."

Jacques smiled, "Later today, I'll take you down to the swimming pool."

"Swimming pool?"

"Yes, I've built a pool just like the Schneiders', so you can practice on the door here."

"Perfect, I see you've thought of everything."

"I try to. Let's not fuck this up."

Mercie was in the kitchen, polishing a silver tea service. Jacques called out to her, and she came into the dining room. "Our friends are hungry, can you bring us something to eat?" He turned to them, "And what are you drinking?"

"I think we'd all like a beer."

"Yes sir," she replied and hurried back to the kitchen.

Jacques had lowered his voice, "She's not too bright, but it's better not to talk in front of her. And put the plans away at night. She'll show you to your rooms after you've had something to eat. And then perhaps you'd like to take a swim?"

CHAPTER FORTY-THREE

JACQUES LEFT THE CHÂTEAU IN the winter morning darkness. The car was warm, the powerful engine silent. He felt the tingle of energy as he thought about his new project. He saw himself examining the artwork, negotiating with the buyers. He sank into the smooth leather seat, and as the strains of Mozart's Jupiter symphony filled the air, he fell asleep.

At sunrise, the sky colorless were it not for the patches of dark gray, Charles-Antoine pulled up in front of La Belle Fermière.

"Come back in an hour," Jacques told him. He didn't care about getting a parking ticket—he never paid them anyway. But the ticket would put him at a precise place and time; he preferred, when possible, to keep his whereabouts unknown.

Most of the faces in the restaurant were familiar—at any rate, the ones that counted. Tanned from skiing or sitting on tropical beaches, they nodded to Jacques with a mixture of fear and distaste. Jacques said hello to a hedge fund manager who had stopped in Paris on his way back to New York City. The man had brought his prized Irish wolfhound along on his holiday. He had chartered a private jet, as he didn't care for his pet to travel in the commercial flight's baggage compartment.

"Good idea," said Jacques, thinking that it was unfortunate that the man paid more attention to his dog than to his wife. For the moment, he'd keep this information to himself.

One of the faces in the restaurant had a grayish sheen: it belonged to Merv Peters. All the energy seemed drained out of him as he slumped in his seat, following but not participating in the conversation at his table.

"Mind if I join you?" Jacques asked as he slid into an empty chair. "Please do," said the others. They had finished their meal, and, one by one, they excused themselves, leaving Merv and Jacques alone.

Merv was quiet, and Jacques found himself in the unaccustomed position of having to make conversation. He had sought out Merv to reassure him that he was researching the provenance of his paintings. It was a way to buy some time. Of course, at some point, he would have to find a permanent solution to the problem, but for the moment, he had other preoccupations.

"How was your holiday?" he asked.

"I spent some time with my sister in the States, and you?"

"Oh, taking care of affairs in Singapore and Montenegro, the usual."

Silence. It looked as though Merv was not going to make this easy.

Jacques tensed the muscles in his cheeks, lifting the corners of his mouth. He looked straight into Merv's eyes in the way that usually impressed upon his listener that he was serious. "I wanted to let you know that I've come across some documents that may help us to establish the chain of ownership for a few of your paintings. I've just gotten back, so it may take me a week or so to sort through them."

He waited for Merv to crack a smile, express his gratitude, but instead, Merv returned his stare with a smirk. "Oh really, yes, I guess you'll have to spend a little time to put it all together. I imagine that it can't be easy, but then, you've had quite a lot of practice, haven't you?"

"Excuse me? I'm afraid I don't understand."

Merv kept his voice low, slowly articulating each word: "You don't understand? That's kind of funny, really. But let me spell it out for you: every painting that I bought from you is either a fake or stolen. You even pulled the same trick on Sauveur Paoli and probably lots of others. I don't know them, but I'll bet I could easily find out. So, here's my offer: you take back the paintings you sold me, refund my money, and I'll keep quiet. Otherwise, I'm going to spread the word on how you defrauded me, and I don't think that even your fancy friends will stick their necks out to save you."

Jacques stood up: "I will attribute your crazy ranting to a bad case of jet lag. But please, Merv, do not threaten me. I will call you in a few days to give you the additional information on the provenance that you've been asking for. Now, you must excuse me, I have a busy day ahead."

# # #

Merv reached for his cup of coffee, it was cold and bitter. Beads of perspiration formed at his temples, his armpits were damp. He had begun to regret his outburst, but it was too late now. He began to rise, but his legs felt weak, and he sat down again. *I need a change of scenery, why not go back to that girl Mag's restaurant?* He would enjoy the drive to Lyon and stay the night; it might even take his mind off the fucking paintings.

# # #

Jacques had started to call Charles-Antoine, but the driver was already there, he had found a parking space right in front of La Belle Fermière. "Just drive around," Jacques told him, I need to be at the club on Rue Saint-Honoré at 12:45."

Michel de Clermont d'Auvergne had asked Jacques to meet him at his club at 12:30. But Jacques believed that being on time—or worse yet, early— was a sign of weakness and insecurity. He always made it a point to arrive late. His nostrils flared, his lower lip stretched over his chin as he thought of Michel. *Fucking snotty aristocrat.* How he despised him and his class. Michel would never invite him to his other club, C2C, no, that was reserved for members of his class. It used to be that you had to have four "noble" grandparents to be eligible for membership. If the rules had loosened a bit, there was still no way for someone like Jacques to buy his way in; it was unlike Michel's club on Rue Saint-Honoré, where new money was welcome.

# # #

Michel had been waiting for Jacques for fifteen minutes when he arrived at 12:45. He found Jacques pretentious and tiresome. Pretentious, because Michel knew of Jacques' humble origins, knew that he had been born Jean-Charles Molina, the son of Portuguese immigrants. Tiresome, because Jacques always arrived late, he seemed to feel that gave him an advantage in his encounters. In contrast, Michel saw it as the posturing of a parvenu. But he had to admit that Jacques could be very useful, he sucked up information like an industrial-strength vacuum cleaner. Even here, Michel was not happy to be seen in Jacques's company, but it could not be avoided.

One of Michel's clients had investments in Brezikstan. The coup d'état had made them nervous, and they had asked Michel what he could find out for them. If Michel found him distasteful, he also knew that, when it came to Brezikstan, there were few people better informed than Jacques. So, he had swallowed his pride, called Jacques, and invited him to lunch. His time was well spent. When it suited Jacques, he could be cold and menacing. However, today he was congenial and volunteered some information that could be useful to Michel's client.

Everyone has ancestors. Michel could trace his family back to a squire in the region of Clermont, who had returned from the disastrous Second Crusade unharmed. His neighbors had not been as lucky. It was thus natural for him to seize the surrounding estates, styling himself as the Chevalier de Clermont d'Auvergne. The family grew in importance with scores of priests, lawyers, judges, and senior advisors to successive governments. With the self-assurance of his class, his breezy familiarity bludgeoned Jacques into submission more effectively than hard words. Had anyone observed the two men, it would have been clear who was the master and who was the servant.

Neither man desired to spend any more time in the other's company. Each had accomplished his objective. For Jacques, it was to further his association with Michel, and for Michel, it was to squeeze information out of Jacques. But convention dictated that they proceed to lunch, which they did before parting company.

CHAPTER FORTY-FOUR

Lyon

ONCE AGAIN, THE BOY LAY in bed in the darkened room. He got up, opened the door gently, and walked soundlessly into the hallway. A shaft of light from a streetlamp illuminated the passage. He went to the toilet, then continued down the stairway, exploring the ground floor of the house. He heard someone coming down the stairs, and somehow he was back in bed. *On a bien dormi, mon petit,* it was the same voice, once more. This time the face came into sharper focus; he could see the thin lips, a broad nose, pockmarked cheeks. He saw the light reflected off the rimless glasses, but when he tried to look more closely, he woke up.

But the dream stayed with him.

Bruno left Sandra's apartment in the inky darkness of an early January morning and walked to the bus stop. An old man with unruly long hair was doing a drunken dance, annoying but harmless. As Bruno approached, the man moved further from the waiting crowd to steer clear of him.

The *Centre d'études* on Rue de l'Observance; he was sure that was the house in his dreams, yet he could not remember how he got there or what he was doing there. But who was the shadowy figure that filled him with dread?

Suddenly, the dormant volcano in his memory erupted spitting out a name: Father Paul. His heartbeat quickened; his intuition told him he would find Father Paul in the house on Rue de l'Observance.

#   #   #

The bus pulled up, and he let the crowd push their way on before him. The old women are the worst, probably just as rude and ugly when they were young as now.

Bruno looked out the window in the direction of the *Presqu'ile*. Now the image of Chez Michel pushed to the front of his mind's eye; he saw Michel, and then he remembered that someone had come asking around for him. That could only be Jacques sending his Brekistan thugs after him. He had taken care of them the last time, and this time he intended to bite off the serpent's head, not its tail.

Bruno thought about other Januarys when he had returned from weeks in Southeast Asia. Hot sun, warm bodies, and drink. Those were the days, but they were over now.

As he disembarked at Quais de Soane, two thoughts collided, twisted together: he needed to confront Father Paul, the face in his dreams, and he needed to kill Jacques Mornnais. He knew it was not the right way to start the New Year, but that was all that he had.

CHAPTER FORTY-FIVE

AS ALWAYS, PARISIAN STREETS WERE clogged with cars, taxis, delivery vans. But Merv was patient—he had plenty of time—and after an hour, he was speeding down the A6 motorway to Lyon. As an occasional car whizzed past, he relived his encounter with Jacques that morning. Should he have vented? It was too late to worry about that now.

He had asked his secretary to cancel his afternoon appointments. In truth, he was bored with his work and the thought of selling his law practice and retiring had gathered momentum. Even if he couldn't sell his paintings, he had set aside sufficient funds to live comfortably. The tableaux remained at the edge of all his thoughts, nibbling like doctor fish, no matter where he tried to direct the ramblings of his mind.

Had he paid more attention to the highway, he might have noticed a white Renault Mégane a hundred meters back. Instead, he concentrated on the road before him. *Maybe my collection is just so much dead skin* he mused, as he turned off the highway and headed towards his hotel in Lyon.

\#   \#   \#

Lyon

It was a year to the day since Marie-Agnès had awakened on an equally cold, overcast morning. She had slapped on some eyeliner and went off to meet Bruno to pick up her check for work she had done for Jacques. In the beginning, things hadn't worked out very well for Marie-Agnès; she was assaulted in the metro, her tote bag stolen, and she wound up in the hospital.

But then Alex, a childhood friend who she'd run into in Parc Monceau, whisked her out of the hospital. While working at Jacques' château, Marie-Agnès had taken some photos of the painters and the atelier where they worked. The two friends feared that Jacques Mornnais, concerned about what Mag had—or had not—seen, was behind the mugging. To protect her friend, Alex had arranged for Marie-Agnès to spend some time with Alex's cousin Charlotte at the house in Trubenne. It was there that she had begun to recover her self-esteem.

Merv Peters, whom she'd met at a cocktail party, invited her to lunch to meet one of his clients, an American heiress named Blondell Royston. Marie-Agnès befriended Blondell, and when Blondell died as the result of a freak accident, Mag inherited her apartment on Place des Vosges in Paris. She sold it and moved to Lyon. Free from financial constraints, she enrolled in a course in restaurant management. While in school, she met a fellow student, Tomas, and together they opened Chez Blondie.

Today, she relived the intense disquiet she had felt that morning a year ago, as she went to meet Bruno. Then she looked around at the restaurant, heard Tomas talking to the staff in the kitchen, and felt a wave of gratitude that, in the end, things had worked out so well, if unexpectedly. Possibly she was not surprised when her eyes skimmed the list of the dinner reservations and saw Merv Peters's name. He was not someone that appealed to her, but he had played a part in the grand scheme of things, and in a way, it was fitting that he chose to dine again at Chez Blondie this evening.

\#   \#   \#

The first thing that struck Merv as he entered the restaurant was the mural on the back wall. Seeing the faces of Jacques and Bruno, even a girl who looked like Marie-Agnès, sent a shiver up his spine. He'd never paid much attention to Tarek and had never met Mila; otherwise, he would have felt even worse. Was the mural there the last time he visited? He didn't remember seeing it, but there they were, staring out from a seventeenth-century painting.

He tried not to look at the mural, but the harder he tried, the more his eyes were drawn to it. It was like trying not to scratch a mosquito bite. The idea of escaping to Lyon had lost its luster, he felt now that his trip had been pointless. Even the quenelles in their delicate sauce failed to lift his spirits out of his socks.

Mag had greeted him briefly when he arrived, and at the end of his meal, she and Tomas came over to his table. "We hope you enjoyed your dinner, was everything all right?"

"Oh quite," he answered absently, his gaze once again focused on the mural. "That mural, it's curious, but I'd swear that I see the faces of Jacques Mornnais and his man Bruno in it. And you're there too, aren't you?"

Tomas laughed, "Yes, that's Marie-Agnès," putting his arm around her shoulders. "She must have inspired the artist, a Polish guy who was passing through. Perhaps he met the other men at some time, who knows?"

So, the two of them were a couple. Well, Mag was not his type anyway, that red hair was a bit scary. He got up to leave: "It's been great seeing you again. And by the way, I saw your friend Carl Weller, I guess we'll see what happens."

A frigid wind stung his face and raised tufts in his thick hair. The bottle of Côtes-Rôtie that he had consumed with dinner made its way in equal parts to his head and his legs. He walked unsteadily to the parking garage, anxious to escape the cold and return to the comfort of his car. *I've had too much to drink,* he thought. He drove slowly out into the street, paying careful attention as he started down the winding hill that led to his hotel overlooking the Saône river.

The incline grew steeper as he progressed, and as he felt the big car accelerating, he put his foot on the brake to slow it down. Nothing happened. He managed to negotiate the first hairpin curve, but the car had picked up speed, and at the next bend, he lost control. The Mercedes flipped over, tumbled down the side of the hill. As it came to rest, flames leaped from the undercarriage. The wind fanned the fire, and soon the car was engulfed in a red fireball that lit up the winter sky. The fire department arrived rapidly, put out the blaze, and extricated Merv from the car. But it was too late; his neck had been broken as the car tumbled down the hillside. An autopsy revealed that Merv's blood alcohol concentration was well over the legal limit, and the cause of the accident was listed as drunk driving.

A white Renault Mégane had been following Merv's car down the hill, keeping a safe distance. The Mégane slowed to watch the car roll down the hill, drove past, and took the road back to Paris.

#   #   #

During the intermission of a performance of Madame Butterfly at the Opéra Bastille, Jacques sipped champagne with a group of traders from a large private bank. It was a purely social occasion, no business was discussed—that would come later. Charles-Antoine was waiting for him as he left the opera house. He settled into his seat for the drive back to the château, remembering with pleasure Butterfly's last aria before she commits suicide. The BlackBerry in his breast pocket vibrated. He read the text message—*SUNSET*—and smiled. It had been a wonderful evening.

CHAPTER FORTY-SIX

Paris

IN THE EARLY MORNING HOURS, the Schneider clan gathered outside their *hôtel particulier.* Six pairs of skis rested alongside a mountain of battered Louis Vuitton suitcases, six pairs of ski boots were lined up neatly at the sidewalk's edge. They went on two ski holidays each winter: once in January when the days were short but the prices low, and again in the spring, when the days were longer. The family, groggy but excited, piled into two minivans that pulled up at the appointed hour. Renaud Schneider turned to look at the gallery as the van moved down Rue de Lisbonne. He felt a twinge of anxiety, but then reassured himself. They had a state-of-the-art alarm system, and their concierge Eduardo Sanchez and his wife Elena would keep an eye on things.

Late afternoon, the pale-yellow sun low on the horizon, Eduardo shuffled out of his small apartment to close the heavy doors leading to the street. At the same moment a tall, well-dressed man hurried in: "Good day, sir, I seem to have locked my cellphone in my car along with the keys, may I use your phone to call for assistance?"

Before Eduardo had a chance to respond, the tall man was already opening the door to his apartment. Elena, sitting at the table, looked up in surprise. Later, she would remember feeling a sharp pain in her forearm before she lost consciousness. Eduardo would recall feeling a prick like the sting of a wasp on his neck before he fell to the floor. The drug had been administered by a second man who had followed his partner into the apartment.

While the first man put out the lights in the apartment and closed the door, his colleague drove a large van into the entrance, locking the *porte-cochère* behind him. Two more men got out of the vehicle, and the foursome proceeded to the back of the courtyard, where they pried open a door leading to the basement.

Once in the basement, following the plans Jacques had provided, they found and disabled the fuse box, cutting off the electricity to the entire building. In the pitch blackness, they donned night vision goggles and made their way to the swimming pool's control room. All went according to plan until they stepped out of the swimming pool area and into the gallery itself. The tall man saw the red blinking light first.

They would have to find the power source for the auxiliary system, and quickly. Someone had to be responsible for turning the alarm on and off, of course. The tall man ran back up the stairs to the concierge's flat, opened the door, and stepped over the two inert bodies. A green light shone on the small console on the wall above Elena's head. He pushed the button to "off," and the console went dark. He ran back down the stairs and through the pool area. The red light was no longer flashing, and they made their way through the gallery, collecting the objects Jacques had identified. They had pushed the plants and deck chairs to the far end of the pool to make room for the collection of commodes, statues, and paintings.

Back up the steps and into the van. While they backed out of the entry, the tall man again entered the concierge's flat. He cut the landline and found the couple's two cell phones. He opened the cell phones, removed the batteries, and threw the phones and the batteries into a nearby garbage bin.

The four men had not uttered a word during the operation, but now, relieved that it had gone well, they laughed and joked. "We were almost fucked, there, weren't we? Good work, Pavel." Ten hours later, the van pulled alongside a dock in the south of France. The goods were loaded on to a ship, that set sail for Jacques' warehouse in Montenegro.

At about the same time, Elena, and then Eduardo came back to the world of the living. Confused, mouths dry, and legs unsteady, they made their way to a building up the street, where they were friends with the concierges. Soon after, the police arrived. The investigation promised to be long and difficult.

CHAPTER FORTY-SEVEN

Château d'Hélène

CHARLES-ANTOINE MADE A QUICK trip to the nearby village, bought *Le Monde, les Echos, le Figaro* and *Paris Match*. After he placed them on Jacques's desk, he went back outside to clear the dead leaves from the lawn in front of the château. Perpetually damp Burgundy: he could feel the rain hovering in the cold wind, but it was better to be out of doors than in the house with Jacques. The man gave him the creeps, the way his eyes stared out from behind his rimless glasses, rarely smiling, ordering Charles-Antoine about in a casual, almost off-handed way. No, despite the shitty weather, he preferred to rake leaves.

Jacques started the morning by reading *Paris Match.* It amused him to compare the stories planted by PR agents with the information in his files. He dropped the magazine to the floor, spread *Le Figaro* out on his desk and let his eyes wander to the large bay windows overlooking the circular drive.

Charles-Antoine was bent over, scooping leaves into a garbage bin. Jacques missed Tarek, but he'd have to make do with his replacement. His eyes moved to the shiny black Mercedes; it reminded him of Merv Peters, he had driven a Merc as well. It was really a pity that Merv had met with such an untimely accident. And Sauveur Paoli, too, was likely to meet with with misfortune. They were both lawyers, it was a dangerous profession. With this thought, his thin lips formed a smile, and a feeling of wellbeing spread out from his abdomen, like a warm caress.

He turned his attention to the newspaper's pale orange *Economie* section. His feeling of wellbeing evaporated as he read the headline, "Smell of scandal surrounds antiques dealers." *Recently retired antique dealer Samuel Greco was arrested by police today in connection with an on-going investigation into the sale of fake eighteenth-century antique furniture. Greco, a well-known figure in the antique furniture world, was accused of working with a group of expert cabinetmakers. They had used original wooden pieces to create perfect copies of eighteenth-century furniture, numbered and stamped with famous cabinetmakers' marks. Greco provided the goods to other well-known antiques dealers, including Renaud Schneider of Maison Schneider. When questioned by the police, Schneider, who had sold a set of chairs—now believed to be fakes—to the Château de Versailles, pleaded his good faith. 'If the government body that approved the sale could not establish that the chairs were fakes, how could I be expected to do so?' The judicial procedure promises to be long and complicated. One wonders if this is an isolated example or the first indication of the massive trafficking of fake objects. Only time will tell."*

A heavy bank of clouds had rolled in, darkening the pale gray sky. The room felt chilly, and Jacques called out to Mercie to bring him some green tea. No one knew that the furniture on its way to Montenegro came from the Schneider gallery. And, under the French legal system, he was sure that the affair would drag on for years; it would soon be forgotten. In any event, if the French government had not been able to spot the fakes, he doubted that his clients in the Gulf would do any better. He remembered Merv telling him that the Schneiders had suffered from a slowdown in the market, thanks to 2008. He wondered if Greco had made them an offer that they couldn't refuse. Still, it angered Jacques to think that he had *trusted* Renaud Schneider, had faith in his honesty. The irony of the situation was completely lost on him.

CHAPTER FORTY-EIGHT

Marseille

CHARLOTTE AND ALEX HAD RETURNED to Marseille. Taking advantage of the mild temperatures and the luminous Mediterranean sky, they sipped their coffee on the little patio at the back of the house. Sauveur called Charlotte later that afternoon, asking if they had returned from Paris. He had just gotten back from a family reunion at La Ciotat. The weather is so splendid, he continued, why don't I show you and your niece the Frioul Islands; even in winter the landscape is pretty amazing.

Charlotte had enjoyed the last sailing outing with Sauveur, and she was eager to accept his invitation. She turned to Alex: "I hope you'll join us, I'm sure you would enjoy yourself."

Alex, thinking about Eugene, looking forward to his call, was less enthusiastic.

"Uh, I think I'll pass.

"Why don't you come and help me in the kitchen? We've always had fun cooking together."

After a dinner of grilled tuna and leek fondue, Alex's mood started to improve, the brain in the gut overriding the heart and the head.

"So, you'll come sailing with us?"

I've got to stop acting like a lovesick teenager, waiting for Eugene to show up. "Well, okay."

They left from the Vieux Port, sailed past the Château d'If, and docked at the marina that connected the islands of Pomègues and Ratonneau. The trio started by exploring Ratonneau, and they returned to the harbor to eat lunch at one of the few restaurants that had remained open in January.

After lunch, they explored Pomègues. Alex climbed—and sometimes had to crawl —up the jagged rocks, photographing the rugged terrain and the hardy vegetation. Later in the afternoon, they returned to the boat.

Alex said she'd like it if they could sail close to the Calanques between Marseille and Cassis, as the sun, now lower in the sky, cast swathes of shadows on the rugged facades. Sauveur turned in the direction of Les Goudes, and at one point, Alex asked if he could stop the boat altogether. Why not, he said with a smile, and they slowly coasted to a halt, bobbing gently in the calm sea.

Alex had moved to the rear of the boat. The camera was in manual mode, and she was so entirely concentrated that she did not hear the speedboat approaching until it was almost level with their boat.

Sauveur and Charlotte were at the forward end of the boat, their arms around each other, talking in low voices, unaware of the speedboat's presence. What made Sauveur twist his head: did he suddenly hear the noise? Sauveur turned to push Charlotte onto the boat's deck. But he was too slow. There were three men in the speedboat, one man steering and the other two raking Sauveur's boat with automatic gunfire. The two lovers fell to the deck, blood streaming from multiple mortal wounds. Alex, startled, turned to face the men, frozen with fear, her finger stuck to the shutter button. She screamed as she ran forward, the speedboat traced an arc in the water and roared off, but not before one of the killers aimed a last burst of fire at her. Blood stained the deck. Alex slipped on the red, sticky puddle and fell, a lone bullet had grazed her shoulder.

It was a Wednesday, school had ended at noon, and a group of adolescents was scaling the Calanque with their instructor, Sylvain Laroni. Later, it seemed to Sylvain that he had heard the noise of the speedboat's engine, the shots, and Alex's cries all at the same time. Hanging off the cliff, he turned to see her screaming and waving her arm. He called the fire department, and they and the gendarmes arrived soon after that. Charlotte and Sauveur were beyond help; Alex, alive but unconscious, was taken to the hospital. The killers' faces were hidden deep in her memory, but it turned out that she had captured their likeness with her camera.

CHAPTER FORTY-NINE

Lyon

DAYBREAK. BRUNO STOOD ON THE right bank of the Saone river, felt the cold wind sweep across the darkness, and inhaled the water's metallic smell. Across the river, the pastel facades were illuminated, swathes of ochre, rose, and yellow in the black sky. With the wind at his back, he started to walk up Montée de l'Observance. The hill was steep, and the road snaked back and forth. By the time he had reached the top, he stopped for a moment to catch his breath before continuing past a row of shuttered buildings.

He came to a halt in front of the *Centre d'études Saint-Bernard*. Two pigeons sat on the low wall that enclosed the garden. As he came closer, they took flight, the wind had died down, and the sound of their wings reverberated in the early morning stillness. For a moment, he imagined that the birds were the souls of lost boys but reconsidered: the boys deserved better than that.

The wind had started up again as he paced noiselessly in front of the Center. He saw lights on the ground floor and in the rooms upstairs. He stepped through the gate, walked up to the front door, and heard the familiar sound of the chimes echoing inside. An elderly priest opened the door. Was he the same man he had seen taking out the garbage some weeks earlier? He couldn't tell.

"Good morning, my son."

"Good morning, Father."

"How can I help you, my son?" asked the priest who remained in the center of the doorway.

"I studied here many years ago with a priest named Father Paul. I'm passing through Lyon, and I wanted to pay my respects. May I come in, please?"

He took a step closer to the old priest, and, although he had not touched him, the man stepped back to one side, and the visitor moved past him. Dim lamps emitted a weak light, casting shadows around the room that smelled of must and old age.

"Where are the boys," asked Bruno, "Still in bed?"

"We haven't had any boys here for years, this is a place for meditation and prayer."

There was a wooden bench pushed against one of the walls, and, without being asked, Bruno sat down. For a moment, he saw a small boy sitting next to him, but when he started to speak to the priest, the boy had disappeared.

"Can you tell Father Paul that I'm here, please?"

"He's resting, he's not well, you know."

"I'm sorry to hear that, I won't be long."

"Please wait here, I'll see if he can receive you."

The visitor had remained seated, but as the old priest started to knock on the door of Father Paul's room, he sensed someone behind him.

"Thank you," said the man as he pushed past him, "I'll just introduce myself now."

The room had once been painted white, but over time, the walls had taken on a greyish cast. It was sparsely furnished: a crucifix on the wall above the bed, a wooden cupboard, a small table, and a chair on which hung a long black robe.

Father Paul, in his pajamas, was reading in bed. His scalp showed through the thin wisps of hair that were combed back from his forehead; his pock-marked cheeks looked waxy in the harsh yellow light of an overhead bulb. A long broad nose, like a bird's beak, traced a line down to his mouth.

He had removed his dentures, and his mouth had collapsed into a fleshy crease. He put his book down on his lap and looked at the visitor through watery pale blue eyes: "Yes?"

The visitor leaned against the door that he had closed behind him. "Good morning, Father, its Bruno, do you remember me?"

Silence. The old priest swallowed, the web of lines around his eyes hardened. "Bruno. I don't recall a boy named Bruno. But that was a long time ago."

"Yes, it was a long time ago. And for a long time, I couldn't— wouldn't—remember how you abused me. I didn't want to remember how you frightened me, how helpless I felt. But one day I had an accident, and I lost my memory. Everything. But when it started to come back, I remembered things that I had forgotten altogether. Like what you did to me."

"I don't know what you're talking about." The old priest breathed deeply; tufts of curly gray hair were visible under the wrinkled pajama top.

A new sensation broke through the surface of Bruno's memory: a wooly chest was pressed against his. "Have you no shame, father?" he asked softly. "How many lives you ruined, you sick old man. The boys you molested, some committed suicide; others are like me, damaged goods. You need to make it right, Father." He sneered as he said the word 'Father.'

"It was so long ago, I'm a different person now."

"Maybe, but you must atone for your sins, isn't that what you told us? A full confession, nothing less will do."

A wave of lassitude rolled over Bruno, submerging his hatred, and leaving him feeling drained. The small room suddenly felt threatening as images from his childhood returned. He had to go: "You can sit at your little table and write it out. I'll be back in a few days."

He pulled open the door to the room, a figure scurried down the hallway—it was the elderly priest who had let him into the house. *He must have heard everything, but so what?*

Bruno returned to Sandra's apartment; he muttered a greeting, went directly to his room, and closed the door. That night, angry thoughts troubled his sleep, anger at the old priest for what he had done. He vowed that tomorrow he would complete what he had set out to do.

CHAPTER FIFTY

NIGHT HAD FALLEN ON MONTÉE de l'Observance, and the darkness wrapped itself around the secrets buried in the undistinguished house sitting behind a withered garden on that street. A run-down ambulance crawled slowly up the street while the passenger looked for the address dictated to him only a short time ago.

The passenger—we'll call him Roger— turned to the driver. His name was Jean-Paul, but everyone called him JP. There was a mole at the tip of his long nose, so it looked like he had a permanent exclamation point etched on his face. "Stop, this is it." JP parked the ambulance on the sidewalk so as not to block the narrow street, and the two men got out of the car, Roger checking a crumpled piece of paper to make sure they were in the right place; it wouldn't do to ring the wrong bell so late at night. But he need not have worried; the front door had been cracked open, the light inside leaking onto the dead branches and brown grass.

An old priest, bent by age, held the door wide open as the two men approached. "Thank you for coming," he mumbled, 'It all happened so suddenly, and I was so worried…"

"No need to worry any longer, Father. We're here to take care of everything. It's part of our job, you know." The man who had spoken—

Roger— looked around the entry and asked, "So where is he?"

"Upstairs, in his room. He's trying to put his affairs in order." Roger turned to JP, "Okay, let's get going. Bring along the suitcase and the bag for garbage, would you?"

They found the object of their late-night visit to Montée de l'Observance seated on his bed. He was breathing heavily, his forehead shone with a grayish sheen under the light of the bare bulb.

"Father, please sit on the chair. We need to strip your bed." The two men worked quickly—this wasn't the first time they'd done this sort of work—and before you could say a prayer, they'd thrown the priest's personal affairs into the suitcase and the bed linens and other junk into the garbage bag. Down the stairs they went, the old man trailing behind them as he painfully descended the stairway. "Anything else?" asked Roger. The priest who'd opened the door led them to the library; "Can you pack all his books and papers into the trunk in the corner?" Roger nodded to his companion, no need to say anything, and he started pulling the old man's books off the shelves.

"Well then, it looks like we're done. We'll leave the trunk here; someone will come by tomorrow to take it away." He returned to the entry, where he saw the old priest, soon to be their passenger, sitting doubled over on the bench. *These old pedophiles all look so frail in the end. Here's another one outrunning his evil deeds.*

"Come with me, Father. We're going to take a little trip. I guess you've done this before, haven't you?"

JP cast a sideward glance at Roger. It wasn't that he didn't share his companion's disgust at what they were required to do. It's just that he kept his thoughts to himself.

#   #   #

JP drove down Montée de l'Observance, turned onto the Quais de Saone, crossed the river, and headed to their destination: a home for retired priests where their passenger would spend the night before continuing his journey. But the following day, instead of being led to a waiting car, the

158

passenger was taken to meet the director of the home. The director had consulted the center's file; his predecessor had met with the passenger many years ago. His brow furrowed, the new director spoke sternly: "So, Father Paul, it looks like once again we have a problem to resolve, smaller this time, I hope. But I don't understand; hadn't we sent you to a church in Aubagne after some people had made a fuss? Why didn't you stay there? What were you doing back in Lyon? And how did that man find you?"

Father Paul fixed his gaze on the new director. It was the gaze of a bird of prey, an old bird, tired, but unwilling to give up. He remembered the previous encounter, but unlike the man facing him, the former director had adopted a conciliatory tone as he sought to defuse the situation.

He was short of breath and spoke haltingly. "So many questions. Let me see. When it was time for me to retire, there was no room for me at the home in Aubagne, and I asked to return to the Saint-Bernard center. There were no longer any boys there, and my request was granted. As to your last question, I have no idea. He told me his name—Bruno—but I don't remember him."

"Did he ask you for money? You'd remember that, wouldn't you?" The director didn't bother hiding his distaste; times had changed, but he still had to follow the old procedures.

"Yes, I mean no, he didn't ask for money." *Of course, I do remember him: Bruno Edremal. But I don't want you digging around and opening old wounds. Please, just send me on my way out of here.*

"All right then. We've arranged for you to live in one of our residences in the southwest. Far enough away from this Bruno. Someplace where you won't be bothered. Just make sure to keep to yourself." He stood up and held the door open for Father Paul, who walked out into the hallway where JP and Roger were waiting for him.

CHAPTER FIFTY-ONE

THE NEXT DAY, AS HE climbed up Montée de l'Observance, Bruno wondered if the elderly priest would even open the door to him. Whatever, he'd find a way to get inside. But it was not necessary: he rang the bell, the door was opened, and the same man greeted once again. Were the two old men the house's only inhabitants, or were there others that he had not yet seen? No matter, he was sure he could take care of himself.

"I've come to see Father Paul, he's expecting me."

"I'm afraid there's some mistake, my son. Father Paul left the center many years ago."

"Don't give me that shit," Bruno shouted and ran up the stairs. The elderly priest stood to one side. Bruno opened the door to the room where he had confronted Father Paul yesterday. The bedclothes had been stripped away; there were no belongings in the open cupboard. Only the faint odor of old age remained.

He stared at the empty room in disbelief. A black curtain closed, and he saw himself lying in the bed. A moment later, the curtain reopened, and the bed was empty. He turned away and returned to the living room in time to see the old priest punching a number into his cell phone. Bruno grabbed the phone, ended the call. "Not so fast. Who might you be calling, Father

Paul, perhaps?" A thick finger pressed into the old man's chest, he fell back, grazed one of the wooden chairs and slipped onto the floor.

"Help me, my son," he said in a weak voice.

Bruno's face was so close to the old man that he could feel the fetid odor of his breath, "Where is he?"

"Too late," mumbled the old man.

"What do you mean, too late?" But the priest had nothing more to say.

Bruno's anxiety had returned. It was not the old man in his death throes that disturbed him but being in the house had brought back layers of hidden memories. His breath came in short spurts, and he sought relief in the chill air. He knew he should return to the house and search for some clue as to the whereabouts of Father Paul, but he could not overcome his growing fear of the place.

#   #   #

Later that morning, a yellow and red van pulled up to the study center. The instructions were to pick up a trunk in the tiny room at the back of the house. The front door was unlocked, and when no one answered, the driver entered the house, where he found the trunk, as well as the lifeless body of the old priest. He loaded the former into his van, called the fire department to report the latter, and left as soon as he could.

He drove down to the Quais de Saone, and although it was midmorning, he walked into a café and ordered a beer. The visit to the house had unsettled him—he had unpleasant memories of catechism classes when he was a child. It wasn't the discovery of a dead body that unnerved him as the realization that he was glad that it was a priest. He felt the need to talk about what he had seen:

"I just came across a dead priest," he said to the man behind the bar.

"Oh yeah?"

"Yeah, I went to a house at the top of the road to pick up the parcel, and there he was, lying on the floor, dead."

"Well, that's life."

The bartender shook his head and continued to load cups and saucers into the dishwasher. The man's discovery was not of any great interest to him, seeing as how people were dropping dead all the time. Bruno, drinking a second cup of coffee to steady his nerves, turned to the man, "A dead priest, you say?"

"Yeah, foul-smelling bugger. Don't care for the clergy much myself."

The bartender looked up, "Yeah, but maybe he was trying to do some good, like sending clothes to needy Africans, you know, something like that."

"You could be right, although I don't know how many Africans there are in the southwest." He sniggered, "Too many if you ask me."

The driver gulped down the rest of his beer; he considered ordering another one, and then thought better of it. He still had a long day ahead of him. "Well, I'll be off. "

Bruno was wondering how he could get a look inside the van when he heard it drive off. *Merde.* Yet he reassured himself: Father Paul was frightened, that was why he had fled. And that was a good thing. *Let him know what it's like to feel afraid.*

Hours later, his train emerged from the tunnel outside Aix-en-Provence. He hadn't finished the job in Lyon, but that was just a temporary postponement. He looked out the window and saw a ribbon of blue glimmering as the sun dropped lower in the sky. While the emotion of joy was unknown to Bruno, at least he felt a faint stirring of satisfaction to be back in Marseille. That was before he heard the news about Sauveur's death.

CHAPTER FIFTY-TWO

Lyon

"I DON'T UNDERSTAND," SAID MARIE-AGNÈS, seated across from her accountant. Félix Germain, like a turtle under attack, had tucked his receding chin into the loose collar of his shirt, leaving her to focus her gaze on his large nose. He shuffled the papers on his desk, looked up, and assumed a neutral posture: eyes vacant, voice low and monotonous.

"For a new business, you've done quite well, in fact. But the government is like a blood-sucking vampire, and they want to get their money before you get to spend your profits. You need to be a bit patient," he ventured.

"Yes, but…..," she began. Tomas gently put his hand on her arm: "It's the way things are, we'll deal with it." Unlike Marie-Agnès, Tomas understood that running a business in France could be a masochistic activity. It certainly was not for the faint of heart.

Félix Germain cleared his throat, "Well, yes, if that's all, we can go over things again in three months," and stood up. He was at home with numbers, regarding humans as a necessary adjunct to his profession. It would not have surprised him if his inter-personal skills were rated 2 on a scale of 10.

Outside the accountant's offices, it had gotten chillier as a wet wind whipped through the bare trees. Marie-Agnès pulled up the hood of her coat; it was a bright red, lined with rabbit fur. *Too flashy, Alex would probably not approve*; she smiled inwardly. It seemed like a lifetime ago since Alex had come to her small studio apartment. She had come to help her to choose her clothes for the fateful forty-eight hours she had spent at Jacques Mornnais' château.

They walked up through *Les Pentes*, stopping in a café for something warm to drink. Marie-Agnès felt uneasy, and then she realized that they were in the café where Bruno had worked. She fought the urge to leave, and at the same time asked Michel, when he brought their hot chocolate, whether Bruno was still working there. "Oh no, he's been gone for a while, but you're not the only one asking after him."

"What do you mean," she asked, but he smiled, shook his head, and shuffled away.

"Are you talking about the same Bruno that…" Tomas started to say.

"You mean, that tried to have me killed? Yes, but never mind, it wasn't personal," she laughed mirthlessly.

Jamais deux sans trois goes the French saying, and Marie-Agnès wondered what other unpleasantness the day had in store for her. She didn't have long to wait.

# # #

She was looking at the papers Félix Germain had given to her, as though staring at them could somehow change what was written. Her phone rang. A small voice said, "Mag, it's me, Alex." Marie-Agnès felt a sharp pain in her belly when she heard Alex's voice, "What's the matter, where are you, are you all right," she asked in one breath.

"No, I'm not all right, Charlotte is dead, and I'm in the hospital," she sobbed.

"Hold on, Alex, tell me where you are, I'm coming right now."

Alex's call had pushed all else to the back of Marie-Agnès's mind. Tomas drove her to Gare Part-Dieu, where she caught the next rapid train to Marseille. She took a taxi to La Timone, the hospital where the firemen had brought Alex. The familiar, slightly cloying smell of antiseptic awakened memories. A wave of nausea rose as she remembered the hospital where she had found herself a year ago. Then her temples throbbed as the image of Blondell, lying unconscious in another hospital bed, crossed her mind. She strode past orderlies, doctors, nurses, women in headscarves, men in djellabas until she found Alex. She was in a room with one other patient; the woman was asleep. The color had washed out of Alex's face; she lay without moving, her eyes open, her gaze devoid of any emotion.

"Oh, Alex," Marie-Agnes leaned over and gingerly pressed her cheek to Alex's, "Tell me again what happened." Alex recounted the events on the boat. "I have no more tears," she said flatly.

Marie-Agnès looked around the room: "I think we should move you, this place is so depressing. I'm afraid I can't repeat what you did last year at Bichat, but where is your doctor, I'll talk to him about getting you out of here."

Their roles were reversed: Alex, always so firm and decisive, lay back on the pillows like a tired rag doll. A year ago, Mag was timid and self-effacing, now she took charge, and the next day Alex was transferred to a private clinic in the Monticelli neighborhood. Here, the corridors were hushed, the room bright, overlooking a tree-lined garden.

"I spoke to my uncle Richard, he's busy making the funeral arrangements. I don't think this has really sunk in yet."

Marie-Agnès asked if she could do anything, but Alex said no, the family was helping to take care of things, it was something that they did well.

"And what about Eugene? Have you spoken to him?"

"Oh Eugene, I think he called when the police were questioning me. Did I tell you, they took my camera?" She gave a wan smile: "I see we have so much in common: hospitals and cameras."

"But what about Eugene, did you call him back?"

"No, I forgot until now; I think they've been pumping me full of drugs to make me sleep."

"If you don't mind, why don't I call him to let him know what happened?"

"Yeah, why not," Alex closed her eyes.

\#   \#   \#

Eugene had returned to Lyon with Travis and Julie at the end of their skiing holiday. He'd called Alex several times, but her phone was always on voice mail. Something was not right. He remembered the day they had met in Paris; he felt that they had put the past behind them, and that Alex was excited that he was coming to Marseille. What could have happened? His phone rang; it was not Alex but Marie-Agnès.

\#   \#   \#

Eugene was at Alex's bedside the following afternoon. Haltingly, she described the day on Sauveur's boat. "The police think the men were after Sauveur and that Charlotte and I were just in the wrong place, wrong time. All I know is what Charlotte told me: that he was an old flame and how much fun she was having seeing him again. It all seems like a cruel trick of fate: why us and why now?"

"I don't know either. I've seen enough senseless death and destruction in my life. But what I do know one thing: fate doesn't take sides."

CHAPTER FIFTY-THREE

Neuilly-sur-Seine

A FEELING OF WEARINESS NAILED Richard to the sofa cushions. He stared at the couch facing him, where Charlotte and Alex had sat, chatting and laughing, only a few short weeks ago. The Vesla de Trubenne family had turned out in force for the funeral. Although they had not seen much of Charlotte over the years, it was expected of them. Richard had waited for a week to pass before scheduling the funeral, to give Charlotte's friends from the Languedoc time to arrange their trip to Paris. They had returned to the apartment in Neuilly after the service at the crematorium. They tried to remember Charlotte but avoided thinking about the circumstances of her death. An invisible barrier kept the groups—friends and family—separate from each other.

Richard wished that Alex could have been there to share the burden of making small talk, but her doctor had said she was still too weak to travel. Erect, and with a gentle smile, he did it on his own. A caterer had served food and drink, and then the mourners started to leave in small clusters, first the family, and then the friends. As for the former, Richard did not regret their departure. He knew they were disappointed. After making a few charitable bequests, Charlotte had left the rest of her estate to Alex. And her shares in Trubenne would pass to the two remaining owners. He thought he heard the word "unfair." And wondered if they were talking about Charlotte's passing or the disposition of her property. No matter, he was not unhappy to see their backs.

It had been awkward when he tried to talk with Charlotte's friends from the south. For them, he was the somewhat cold, patrician banker who until recently had visited Trubenne only on occasion. As for Richard's own friends, he had outlived most of them, and the survivors, like Michel de Clermont d'Auvergne's father Arnaud, were too feeble to attend.

Richard now stared at Michel, who had come to pay his respects. The bags under Richard's eyes looked like two purple balloons, the skin around his neck sagged, and Michel noticed a slight tremor in his hand as he placed his drink on the coffee table. Today, Richard was starting to look his age.

"What a nasty business," Michel said.

"Yes," sighed Richard, "I still don't understand what happened. Maybe you have some idea?"

"Not for the moment, but I can try to find out."

Michel stood up, "Please, don't get up, I can find my way out," but Richard had slowly and painfully risen, and walked him to the door.

#   #   #

A few days later, Alex was discharged from the clinic and was told to take it easy. She called Richard and announced that she was coming to Neuilly to see him. Eugene, who didn't want her to make the trip alone, accompanied her. She was dressed in black, not a sign of mourning, but she simply couldn't be bothered to think about clothing. Her blond hair was pulled back from her face; there were bluish circles under her eyes, and the stress and fatigue had stretched her skin tightly across her cheekbones. Eugene thought that she looked the same, and yet different. He had seen it before, how a tragedy etched itself onto the faces of those left behind.

Richard led Alex and Eugene into his study, where he had placed the urn with Charlotte's ashes. Her eyes glistened, not with tears but with anger.

"Why, why," she asked, her arms held rigidly by her sides, the fists clenched. "I know it sounds far-fetched, but do you think this had anything to do with Jacques Mornnais looking for me?"

Richard spoke up. "I'm meeting Michel at my club this afternoon; he said he wanted to talk with me. I won't stop until I find the answers to your questions."

#   #   #

It wasn't the icy wind and the freezing temperatures. Richard had always walked to the Pont de Neuilly and rode the métro to the Concorde station. But today, gripped in the jaws of weariness that wouldn't let up, he called a taxi to take him to Rue Boissy d'Anglas. He had begun to find the atmosphere in his apartment stifling, and he looked forward to the familiar, comforting surroundings of his club. At least there the world was as it had always been. Standing in front of the C2C's carved wooden doors, he threw his shoulders back and lifted his chin as he rang the bell—his self-esteem wouldn't let him do otherwise.

He nodded to the few faces that he recognized, and without stopping went to sit opposite Michel de Clermont d'Auvergne. Seeing Michel reminded Richard that things were, in fact, not the same. You could have all the rules and regulations you desired, but the adage, "like father, like son," didn't always hold true. The Clermont d'Auvergne family could trace their ancestors back to the Second Crusade. Still, there was a weakness about Michel, something tentative in his regard. A thought formed in Richard's mind—*he's like an eighteenth-century gentleman caught in the twenty-first century* —and he smiled.

Richard lowered himself into the dark brown leather club chair. Michel asked how he was feeling, "We're all distraught, I think you know that, and I was hoping you could shed some light on what happened." Richard hadn't meant to snap, but there was no point in beating around the bush: either Michel had something to tell him, or he didn't.

A waiter brought their order—green tea for Richard and another espresso for Michel. After the waiter walked off, Michel took his time, sipping his coffee, staring into the small porcelain cup. Richard waited, he felt that Michel was trying his patience, but he said nothing. At last, Michel looked up: "We are quite convinced that Charlotte was collateral damage, she happened to be in the wrong place at the wrong time. The same is true for Alex." His gaze returned to his coffee cup.

"So, what was happening at that time and place? Dammit, Michel, don't make me ask you questions! If you know something, then tell me. If not, stop wasting my time."

"The only thing I know is that at least one of the killers came from Brezikstan, it's a small country…"

"I am familiar with Brezikstan, Michel. But what was this man Saveur Paoli mixed up in? Why did they kill him?"

"I don't know, but if I hear anything, I'll let you know."

CHAPTER FIFTY-FOUR

Paris – earlier in the week

MICHEL HAD FOUND CHARLOTTE'S DEATH troubling. He invited Kenneth Petit, his former colleague at the DGST, to meet him for lunch at his club on Rue Saint Honoré. It was personal, not business, he said by way of explanation. Over the years, the two men traded rumors and bits of gossip; Michel, nagged by feelings of inadequacy, Kenneth, resentful of Michel's privileged status: inherited, not earned.

"It's about Charlotte, she was the cousin of Richard Vesla de Trubenne, the banker."

"Yes, terrible situation."

"The family is in a state of shock, they don't understand what happened. I thought you might have an idea."

Kenneth cast his eyes around the dining room, took in the self-satisfied faces of the ruling elite, heard the buzz of discreet chatter, the clatter of flatware on porcelain plates. On the one hand, he didn't care much about the fate of one aging aristocrat, and yet, on the other hand, that was precisely what he was paid to do. Kenneth took his time, slicing off a morsel of perfectly done entrecôte. He brought the fork to his mouth and chewed, savoring the flavor, and giving himself time to decide how much he would tell Michel.

"I can't tell you very much. We think the killers—or at least one of them—were from Brezikstan. "

"Brezikstan…Isn't Jacques Mornnais their man on uranium deals?"

"Indeed."

"But what does that have to do with Sauveur Paoli, or with Charlotte, for that matter?"

"We have no idea. But our guess is that the target was Sauveur; the two women were in the wrong place at the wrong time."

It depressed Michel to realize that Kenneth was holding out on him. The mention of Jacques Mornnais's name said it all, but it got him to thinking.

CHAPTER FIFTY-FIVE

BABS TOMASON EAGERLY ANSWERED THE phone when she saw "Michel CA" flash on the screen. She had invited Michel de Clermont d'Auvergne to her get-togethers any number of times, but he was frequently already tied-up. While he had impeccable manners, there was also something standoffish about him. Well, what could one expect from someone with his lineage?

"How are you, Babs?"

"Michel, how lovely to hear from you. I'm just fine, thanks, and you?"

"Oh, making do, I guess. You had mentioned that you were having some people over tomorrow, and I wonder if I might join you. I thought I'd be visiting my father, but it turns out I'll be in Paris after all."

"Of course, you must join us. Such a pleasure."

"The pleasure will be mine, dear lady."

Michel looked forward to the gathering. It was not the company that interested him—Babs and her friends were such social climbers. Instead, he hoped to provoke Babs into gossiping about Jacques Mornnais. However, things didn't go as he had planned.

He had intended to arrive early and talk to Babs before her other guests arrived. But a demonstration of theatrical personnel, demanding an increase in their unemployment benefits, tied up traffic at Porte Maillot. When he stepped out of the elevator, he saw that he'd have to find a way to get Babs away from her guests. Either that or stay until everyone had left, which he dreaded.

Babs introduced him as her dear friend Michel de Clermont d'Auvergne. He felt like a prize-winning cow at an agricultural fair, but he took it in stride and waited for the right moment. It came when Babs ducked into the kitchen to tell the maid to bring out more hors d'oeuvres. He followed her, gently held her elbow, and said: "Can I have a private word with you, Babs?"

"Of course, Michel," she said, moving so close to him that he could feel her breath and the warmth of her body (which did not interest him in the least).

"My family, we've been talking about investing in some artwork, and I think you mentioned that man, what was his name, an art dealer that you know?"

"Oh, you mean Jacques Mornnais. I haven't seen him in a while, but I could give you his phone number, you could call him and say that you know me."

"Thank you, dear lady. That would be so helpful. Do you know if he's in Paris right now?"

"I don't know." She thought for a moment. "Did you ever meet Merv Peters, the lawyer? He told me that he was going to ask Jacques for help in selling his collection. He died in a terrible automobile accident last week, and I don't know if he ever got to see Jacques or not."

A parenthesis in time opened: Babs looked down at Michel's shoes (J.C. Westin, not new, with a dull sheen), observed his tweed jacket (Arnys, a bit wrinkled). And noticed his smooth rosy cheeks (he had shaved just before coming over). Michel looked straight ahead, not breathing. Then the parenthesis closed. "No, I'm afraid I never met the gentleman. So sorry," he said, and left Babs to tend to the hors d'oeuvres.

Michel sidled up to three women who were standing in front of the buffet table. "Pardon me, please," he murmured as he reached for a verrine filled with a purée of something green. It wasn't hard to eavesdrop on their conversation; they spoke in that animated way that was typical of so many Americans.

"Poor Merv Peters," one of them was saying.

"Excuse me, I couldn't help overhearing you. I met Merv Peters once, what happened to him? Forgive me, I'm Michel de Clermont d'Auvergne, and you?"

Three pairs of eyes did a quick head to toe examination, registered his pedigree, and responded at the same time. Michel learned that friends of theirs had seen Merv at La Belle Fermière the very day that he had had his accident. It turned out that he'd been having a discussion with a well-known art dealer. What kind of accident? He'd lost control of his car and drove off the road. Terrible. Yes, perhaps he'd had too much to drink with dinner. One had to be so careful.

He chatted with the women for a few minutes longer, until he could politely leave, pleading another engagement. Michel decided to walk home from Babs' place. A wave of relief swept over him. He had escaped the overheated apartment; he'd left the heady mixture of perfume and the aroma of the food behind him. He tightened the muffler around his neck to block the cold, damp night air. He needed a good, long walk to clear his mind and to sort things out.

It was almost eleven p.m. by the time he returned to his home on Rue de Varenne. He walked past the policemen guarding Hotel de Matignon and the Italian Embassy; how much more difficult if not impossible it was to guard against hidden dangers.

The next morning Michel called Kenneth Petit. He had learned about the death of Merv Peters, who had been seen with Jacques Mornnais the very day he died. Surely Kenneth knew that. It was clear that Jacques Mornnais was the common factor in the two men's deaths. Why was he playing him for a fool?

"I'm sorry, Michel, but I can't say anything more. You understand, I know. I'm genuinely sorry, but I've got to leave for a meeting. Let's meet for lunch next week, I'll call you. "

Kenneth Petit felt a tinge of annoyance. On the one hand, Michel could be such a pain in the ass at times, but on the other hand, the man had his uses. Kenneth turned to Michel when he needed to pierce the circle of the tight-knit aristocracy. Over lunch, Kenneth would ask for Michel's help, and in return, he'd let slip some compromising information during their meal. Pumping up the man's self-importance was a small price to pay for a new contact.

As for Jacques Mornnais, he was getting to be a pain as well. Two murders in one week, the man was coming unhinged. Kenneth wondered how much longer Jacques's protectors would put up with him. While his services were undoubtedly valued, no one was irreplaceable. Lately, Jacques seemed to have forgotten that truism.

CHAPTER FIFTY-SIX

Fresh Meadows & Paris

EARLY EVENING. PHYLLIS PETERS WAS smoothing the wrinkles out of a piece of aluminum foil when the call came. She saved tin foil, reused paper towels as napkins, and scooped up packets of sugar, mustard, and ketchup whenever she could. *Why am I doing this* Phyllis asked herself during rare moments of self-awareness. But as she was not really looking for an answer, she continued to practice the pointless frugality that cluttered drawers and the countertop.

Her brother had, sadly, perished in an automobile accident, said the caller. He was a lawyer, one of Merv's colleagues in Paris, and the executor of his will. Phyllis asked if he could ship the body back to the United States for burial. After the funeral, she would arrange to come to Paris as soon as she could. Tears rolled down her cheeks, plopped on the now smooth piece of tin foil. She felt a surge of anger at the suddenness of it all as she remembered how on edge Merv had been when he visited at Christmas.

The next day, after school let out, she hurried to the bank, sat at a grey metal table in the safe deposit vault, and leafed through the papers Merv had left. Each set of documents dealt with a different painting, and she assumed that these were part of the collection her brother had spoken about. But Phyllis couldn't see what this had to do with his irritability. She returned the papers to the safe deposit box, went home, and heated up a frozen dinner.

The prospect of a trip to Paris filled Phyllis with trepidation. Not much of a traveler, she'd been to the Dominican Republic and the Virgin Islands on short vacations, but she had never crossed the Atlantic. Flying to Paris, meeting with the lawyer, she'd have to go through the belongings in his apartment, and hadn't he mentioned a house in the country? It seemed overwhelming. She ruminated over the weekend, and Sunday afternoon, she called Sylvia. Would she like to come to Paris with her? They could stay in Merv's apartment—it was a duplex and apparently quite extraordinary. And Sylvia could view his collection.

Sylvia was ecstatic. Unlike Phyllis, she had no fear of the unknown. She had been wondering how much longer she would live in Fresh Meadows, and the invitation opened a whole new field of possibilities. Phyllis was understandably in a fragile state of mind, and Sylvia would offer all her energy to help her settle Merv's estate.

A month later, Phyllis and Sylvia flew to Paris. The executor—a lawyer named Russell Denton—was waiting for them at the apartment on Rue Le Sueur. He pointed to two keyrings on a small table in the entry. These are the keys to the apartment and your brother's house in the country."

"Thank you. I was meaning to ask…"

Russell Denton interrupted her: "I'm sorry, but I've got to run; I'm already late for a meeting." Phyllis stood frozen in place, wondering what to say. Did he expect her to apologize for taking up his time?

As the lawyer pivoted towards the door, he added, almost as an afterthought, "Why don't you try to get some rest now? I'll see you at my office tomorrow at 10 o'clock, and we can go over everything."

The door closed. "Well I never," exclaimed Sylvia and having said all that there was to say, the two women began to explore the apartment. As they did so, Phyllis understood why Merv always seemed anxious to leave when he visited Fresh Meadows. Fine furniture, expensive bibelots, the windows hung with heavy drapes. It had occurred to her that he'd never invited her to visit; she guessed he felt she didn't fit into his luxurious Paris life. "Pretty nice," said Sylvia, as she touched the upholstery, fingered the drapes, gently examined a gilt and porcelain clock on a marble-topped commode. "So, where's his famous collection?"

"Oh, that. Let's look upstairs."

Phyllis opened the door and stepped inside Merv's secret garden. She was speechless. Not that she felt blown away by the beauty of the paintings, but rather because she didn't know what to think. Merv had mentioned his collection, but it was a word empty of meaning for her. Looking at the paintings, she felt no connection to them, and she wondered why Merv had decided to become a collector. Perhaps it had something to do with status, she couldn't be sure.

Sylvia walked around the room, examining the nineteenth and twentieth century works. She noticed a blank space on the wall above the door, breaking the silence: "What's that, it looks like he must have sold that one." But Phyllis was staring at Bernard Buffet's signature on the painting that Jacques had sold to Merv to replace the one that had been stolen. Merv's records were in alphabetical order, and she thought she had seen that name when she sat in the bank's vault. When Phyllis heard Sylvia's voice, she knew that her companion had accompanied her not so much as an act of friendship but on account of the collection. *That's okay*, she thought, *we'll each get what we want out of this trip.*

They descended the stairs, each lost in her thoughts. Phyllis saw a pile of delivery service menus on the buffet. "How about some sushi," she asked Sylvia. Five minutes later she had called the number on the brochure and ordered.

They unpacked the large bag of food in the kitchen. This space was not for show; the paint on the walls needed freshening, the table and chairs were functional but ugly, the bare bulb cast a harsh light. Phyllis imagined Merv sitting in the kitchen, alone in the big apartment, and to her surprise, she felt sorry for him. Sylvia concentrated on manipulating her Maki and avoided any mention of the paintings again this evening.

#   #   #

A dark, gray morning, needles of freezing rain pounding the windows. Phyllis had been up long before sunrise. She showered, dressed, and poked around the kitchen, searching for something to eat. She found a jar of instant coffee of uncertain age, boiled some water, and forced herself to drink the hot, tasteless liquid. *At least this will keep me awake.* Sylvia entered the kitchen, "Ugh, that smells awful." "It's the best I can do for breakfast." "Throw that shit out. Let's go to a café and have a real French breakfast."

"Of course, why didn't I think of that?"

"That's what friends are for, sweetie."

The croissants, accompanied by butter and jam, provided a pleasant albeit temporary feeling of wellbeing, enough to get them through the meeting with the executor.

CHAPTER FIFTY-SEVEN

Paris

RUSSELL DENTON STUDIED THE TWO women surreptitiously as he fiddled with the papers on his desk. He'd only spent a few minutes with them yesterday, and now he had a chance to observe the pair more closely. Phyllis, Merv's sister, was a drab woman, in need of a good layer of subcutaneous fat. She wore a cream-colored blouse under her shapeless black suit. He glimpsed sensible walking shoes, noted the dull black patina. Her companion reminded him of a massive bird—*was there such a thing as a massive bird,* he wondered. She was a study in tones of burgundy and gray. Various gradations of the two colors decorated her full skirt, blouse, what he thought might be a vest, and a short-sleeved jacket. She had completed her outfit with a black hat, perched on a mass of unruly gray hair. He noticed that she, too, had opted for sensible footwear: black high-top sneakers. They made quite a couple, but he composed his face into a serious yet caring mien. After all, the mousy one had inherited some substantial property, and he would do his best to help her.

He spent the requisite time talking about what a wonderful man Merv Peters had been, and how shocked the ex-pat community had been by the news of his death. He pivoted quickly to the business at hand. Merv had left several bank accounts, and he estimated that once all the bills had been paid, there might be a little over one million Euros remaining. Not a fortune, but nothing to sneeze at either. In addition, her brother had left two valuable properties: the duplex apartment where they were staying, and a country home in Normandy. And, of course, there was his collection of artworks.

As Merv's executor, he'd be handling all the tedious administrative work—we're in France, I'm sure you've heard about the impossible bureaucracy—and of course, taxes. Speaking of taxes, it would be necessary to sell some of the assets to pay the bill; he'd let her think about that, no need to decide today. Just then, Phyllis's sugar high crash-landed, leaving her to feel the full effects of jet lag. "May I have a glass of water, please?"

Sylvia spoke for the first time. Hadn't Merv left a very valuable collection? Surely Phyllis could sell some of the paintings to pay the tax collector. "Of course," replied Russell Denton, or she could make a donation to the French state. "We'll need to examine all your options carefully, but we need to begin by getting an appraisal."

Phyllis drained the glass of water, waited for her hands to stop trembling. "I think I'd like to rent a car and visit the country house tomorrow. You wouldn't by any chance be able to give me directions?"

"Indeed I can, dear lady," and he pushed a pale yellow sheet of paper with a map and directions across his desk. Phyllis stood up, she felt steady on her feet now.

"Thank you so much. I'm afraid that this is all a bit much, and I need to think about everything you've told me. Can I call you in a few days?"

#   #   #

The driving rainstorm had let up, replaced by a wet mist that rendered hair and clothing soggy and limp. Phyllis felt that the mist had entered her brain as well, soaking the nerve endings and making thought difficult. Nevertheless, she managed to drive to Neuilly-sur-Seine, where they picked up the motorway to Normandy. Two hours later, they entered the village of Saint-Germer-de-Fly. After driving around in circles for another fifteen minutes, they found the small road, really nothing more than a paved path, which led to Merv's country house.

They turned onto the gravel drive outside the barn, the mist lifted, and as a reward for their patience, millions of tiny droplets on the lawn shimmered in brilliant sunshine. Phyllis jumped out of the car, strode through the tall, wet grass, and unlocked the front door. Inside, the air smelled cold and damp. She opened the shutters, the sunlight falling on the wooden sideboard, the comfortable-looking sofa, and easy chairs. She realized that the room reminded her of their childhood home in Fresh Meadows. *This is the real Merv*, she thought.

Sylvia stepped into the room, sniffed, "This place smells," she said.

"Oh, it just needs to be heated."

Merv had never bothered to turn off the electricity, and soon the radiators took the chill off the room. As well, the women found a surprisingly well-stocked freezer.

Phyllis and Sylvia sampled some of her brother's prized Calvados. "I'm certain he had been more at home here than in his luxurious duplex," Phyllis confided to Sylvia. Another sniff, Sylvia's way of expressing disapproval.

"Do you really think so? I mean, what is there to *do* here besides watch the grass grow?"

"I don't know. It just seems so beautiful and peaceful. That counts for something, doesn't it?"

The next morning, Phyllis didn't move from her bed: mouth dry, tongue thick, she waited for the throbbing in her head to subside. While she grappled with the consequences of drinking too much aged Calvados, Sylvia was already dressed.

"There's an ancient Abbey in the town, shall we go take a look?" she called out, her voice like a spear piercing her friend's closed eyes. "Later," she mumbled and went back to sleep.

Sylvia turned on the television. "This is CNN," said a familiar voice. She watched the news for ten minutes—it was like being back in Fresh Meadows. This was not why she had agreed to accompany Phyllis. Sylvia left her friend to sleep off her hangover, drove into the town, walked around, and toured the Abbey.

By the time Sylvia returned, Phyllis was sitting in the living room, drinking tea. She, too, had turned on the television, but unlike Sylvia, she liked the comfort of the familiar. Phyllis put on her sunglasses—her eyes still ached—went outside and enjoyed the feeling of walking through the wet grass, the chill running up her legs. She walked over to the barn. It looked like Merv had used the space as a kind of attic. There were boxes of magazines, an old computer, some broken chairs, old suitcases, garden implements, a lone ski pole, large cans of paint.

As Phyllis gazed around the barn, a thought came, releasing the pain behind her eyes, giving her a feeling of wellbeing. She would live here during her long summer vacation; she would clear out the barn, turn it into one, maybe even two studios, and rent them out. She felt sure that Merv would have wanted it to be this way, and she smiled for the first time since she had learned of her brother's death.

Back in the house, she removed her wet shoes and socks, found a towel, and sat down to dry her feet and legs. Sylvia was leafing through some art books.

"What's that," asked Phyllis.

"I found a pile of *catalogues raisonnés* over there," Sylvia said, pointing to a small room that Merv had used as her office. "All of them seem cover the painters in his collection, except this one—it's a listing of works by Picasso. I don't think your brother had a Picasso, did he?"

"I'd like you to put those books back where you found them, Sylvia."

"Well, I hope you don't think I...."

"I don't think anything. But let's have some lunch and head back to Paris. I've seen what I needed to see."

"Oh, so I guess you're going to sell this place?"

"No, I'm going to sell the apartment, it's very nice, but it's not for me. And I doubt that I could afford the upkeep. I have some plans for this place. And, Sylvia, don't worry, if and when I sell the paintings, I'll ask you to help me."

CHAPTER FIFTY-EIGHT

La Ciotat

SAUVEUR'S FUNERAL CEREMONY TOOK PLACE in La Ciotat, the small church gleaming white against a cloudless blue sky. The Mayor of Marseille was seated at the front, right behind the members of the immediate family. The church was filled to overflowing with Sauveur's many business associates, friends, and his large extended family.

Bruno hadn't intended to go—funerals were for the living, and he hardly knew those who would be attending—but at the last minute, he changed his mind. Perhaps he owed this to Sauveur, after all. Bruno hunched over his motorcycle, the cold wind blowing down from the northwest. As he approached La Ciotat, he saw the sea dotted with white caps. *If only the wind had been blowing like this, Sauveur would not have gone sailing,* he thought.

After the funeral service, he followed the hearse and the cavalcade of cars and limousines out to the cemetery, where he stood at the back of the crowd as Sauveur's coffin was lowered into the ground. He noticed a young woman, a bit too made-up, showing a bit too much perfect leg, one version of Mediterranean beauty. Bruno recognized the older woman who accompanied her. This one definitely not a beauty—never was, never would be—but she had come to Sauveur's office to confirm that his prized Signac painting was a fake.

The burial completed, the crowd started to disperse. Several of the men hovered around Stephanie Amelinni, drawn to her, as the saying so aptly describes it, like flies to shit. But when Maud Cousin mentioned how they came to know Sauveur, all attention turned to her. One of the men, sunglasses perched on a perfectly shaved and sun-tanned head, said he and Sauveur were related and had sailed together. He was tall, barrel-chested, and he had a winning smile. The man handed his card to Maud Cousin and said he hoped she wouldn't mind if he came by the Burlotti, perhaps they could go out for a coffee. He could feel Stephanie's eyes on him, but this was business.

Bruno passed the group as he headed towards his motorcycle. It was Maud and not the girl who was the center of attention, and he knew the reason why immediately. He imagined that by tomorrow everyone in Marseille would know that Sauveur had been swindled. It wouldn't take much to connect the dots. Bruno had his own reasons to want Jacques Mornnais dead: he'd need to hurry to the head of the line.

CHAPTER FIFTY-NINE

February 2011

Fresh Meadows, New York

PHYLLIS WAS WALKING HOME FROM school when the tears welled up. Sniffling, she stopped to fish around in her bag for a tissue—she needed to wipe the tears away before anyone saw her. It was so frustrating; Phyllis would be doing something, even looking after the children during recess, and the tears would start to flow. *Why?* she asked herself. She hadn't been close to her brother. There hadn't been much affection between them, only the shared memories of their dull, uneventful childhood. And then he'd left for Paris. He had made a name for himself, had mostly forgotten about her and Fresh Meadows except when it suited him to remember. So, why was she crying?

When she got home, she prepared a cup of tea—she hoped it would make her feel better. She took off her sensible shoes and put on her slippers. With a sigh, she undressed and put on her pajamas and bathrobe. Seated at the kitchen table, she sipped her tea and wondered if it was too early to go to bed. It was four p.m.

The phone was ringing. Phyllis let it ring; she didn't feel like talking to anyone right now. An hour later, it started to ring again. *Those damn telemarketers, they'll just keep calling until I answer.*

She didn't feel like being polite: "Yes, what do you want?" Silence. "Why are you bothering me?"

"Excuse me, *Madame*, may I speak to *Madame* Peters, please?"

It was not a telemarketer, after all. The woman at the other end of the line had spoken in English but with a foreign accent. Phyllis's hostility drained out through her teary eyes. "I'm sorry, I didn't mean to snap. I'm Ms. Peters, and who are you?"

"No, it is I who am sorry to disturb you, *Madame*. I'm calling from the office of Russell Denton, the executor of the estate of Mervin Peters. Mr. Denton would like to speak with you."

"Oh, yes. Of course."

Phyllis blew her nose, took a sip of tea, as the assistant transferred the call. "Hello Ms. Peters, I hope you are well? Is this a good time to talk?"

No, it's not. "Hello Mr. Denton, yes, this is a fine time to talk."

"Very good. Well, let me get to the point, Ms. Peters. I'll start with the good news. It's early days still, but I think that your potential tax liability will be much lower than I had originally imagined."

"Oh? Yes, that *is* good. But you said you'd start with the good news, so I guess you've got some bad news for me as well."

"Well, yes. You remember that I said we'd need to get the paintings in your brother's collection appraised? I contacted a well-known expert, someone we can trust to do the right thing, you know, and well, not to put too fine a point on it…" *Will this man never get to the point?* "…it would seem that many of the paintings in the collection may not be originals."

"Do you mean that they are fakes?"

"Uh, yes, we have to consider that possibility."

"But couldn't your appraiser be mistaken? What I mean is, how sure is he that the paintings are not originals?"

"Not 100%, that's the thing. The appraiser says without knowing the provenance, he cannot say for certain. So, I was wondering if you might have any of your brother's papers. We checked the files in his office, there was nothing helpful."

"Um, I need to think about that. Can I call you back?"

"Why, of course, Ms. Peters."

The tea was cold; she boiled water and used the same tea bag to make another cup. She looked at the kitchen clock; it was too late to go to the bank today, but she'd stop by as soon as she got out of school tomorrow.

#   #   #

Once again, she sat at the gray metal table in the bank vault. Previously she had flipped rapidly through the files, wondering why Merv had been so on edge. She examined them more carefully this time and thought that she understood what had been bothering her brother.

She had brought a notebook with her; it had a hard, black-marbled cover, the kind grammar school children used for their lessons. She noted the contact information for Nicolas Pagès, the gallery owner from whom Merv had bought his paintings. On the bottom of the drawer, under the files, was a sheet of yellow lined paper, torn from a legal pad. She recognized Merv's sloppy handwriting and managed to decipher what he had written: another name and phone number were scrawled at the bottom of the page. She copied them down as well.

The safe deposit box was in her name; she had opened it at Merv's request when he had come for a quick visit in September. *The box belongs to me, and I'll bet that no one knows that I have Merv's records.* She looked at her watch; it was almost five p.m. That would be 11 p.m. in France; it was too late to call tonight, but she'd make her calls tomorrow morning.

#   #   #

She called Nicolas Pagès first. A woman answered the phone, and Phyllis hoped she understood English as she introduced herself: "Hello, my name is Phyllis Peters, my brother was one of Mr. Pagès's clients, and I'd like to speak to him please."

Véronique answered in English, but her answer dashed Phyllis's hopes: "I'm sorry, but I cannot help you. My father is deceased."

Not to be deterred Phyllis pushed on ahead: "I'm sorry for your loss, but my brother bought some paintings from him, and I was wondering if you have any records…."

"What did you say your name was?" interrupted Véronique.

"Phyllis Peters, my brother was Merv Peters, he died in a car accident last month."

Véronique took a deep breath: "I am sorry, Madame Peters, but I have no records. And I am quite busy at this moment, so please forgive me, but I must go."

Phyllis gave a start as Véronique ended the call. The woman had been so rude, but she hoped to have better luck with the next name on her list.

\#   \#   \#

Jacques wasn't expecting a call from the United States, and when the number flashed on his BlackBerry screen, he let the phone ring until it switched to voice mail. Ping, the caller had left a message:

"Mr. Mornaize, my name is Phyllis Peters. You advised my brother Merv Peters to purchase some paintings, and we need to talk about that, now that my brother is deceased. Can you call me back, please?"

CHAPTER SIXTY

Lyon

SANDRA HAD STARTED DRINKING AT breakfast several weeks ago. It hadn't been easy. Usually, she stopped in a café on her way to the bank, ordered a *tartine* and a *café crème*. She began by adding a single glass of wine—it was all she could stand. Over the next weeks, she managed to down two glasses at breakfast. Next, she cut down on the bread and coffee, so that she was tipsy by the time she arrived at work. The smell of the cheap red wine made her nauseous, it stained her lips red and darkened her teeth. But she persevered.

When she reached the bank, her first stop was the kitchen, where she made a double dose of espresso to counter the effects of her early-morning tipple. Her colleagues cast furtive glances as she slowly picked at the keys of her computer. They had grown more remote since Sandra had been reprimanded for her carelessness in allowing Caroline Trabert to access her computer. It was as if her negligence was a disease that could be transmitted by close contact, so they kept their distance. No one ventured to ask if anything was wrong, or if they could help. Sandra had never had any illusions that the people she worked beside were her *friends*. But, embittered by the way they had cut loose from her so quickly she stopped acknowledging them at all.

One morning, a vibration passed through the back office. It was as if all the air had been sucked out of the room. The imposing silhouette of Cyril de la Forêt du Maine—bulging midriff and drooping eyes—made its appearance. It was only on rare occasions that the President of the ATB Bank visited the lower orders. But, having received reports on Sandra's behavior, he felt he had to see for himself.

"Good morning, Sandra," his voice boomed with the forced joviality of an amateur actor. One of her hands gripped her chin to hold her head up, the other rested on her desk. She slowly raised her gaze from the computer screen to the President's face, his features now frozen into an ugly grimace.

"Oh, good morning, Cyril," she whispered, too tired to raise her voice. Cyril took a deep breath, preparing to speak. Wine, coffee, and perspiration: he inhaled the unpleasant mixture.

"Sandra, I think you need to follow me, please."

She rose, "Sure." A cloud of her body odor, now stronger, caught up with him as she followed on his heels. The Human Resources Director was already in Cyril's office.

"Please, Sandra, take a seat, this won't be long."

Cyril nodded to the HR Director; he would be the one to do the talking. "As you know, Sandra, we were very disappointed by how Caroline Trabert was able to access your computer. After a thorough investigation, we concluded that while you were very negligent, you were not complicit, and we allowed you to continue to work for the bank. But despite our bending over backward—and I cannot emphasize enough how kind we've been—you've now put us in an impossible situation. I'm talking about your coming to work drunk every day. I'm sure you understand that under the circumstances, you cannot remain employed by the bank."

Sandra had lowered her head. It was as though she was about to receive a blessing, or a pat on the head for work well done. Her eyes were cast downward, focused on the pattern in the Oriental rug on the floor beneath Cyril's desk. The HR Director must have taken her silence for acquiescence, for he continued:

"You realize, of course, that we could fire you for cause, and you wouldn't get a penny. But given your long years of service, until the incident with Madame Trabert and this…uh, current situation, we're prepared to make what I think you will agree is a generous offer. You agree to resign, and we agree to pay you an indemnity. It's not a large amount of money, but still, more than you would expect, given the circumstances. You'll still be entitled to your unemployment insurance, by the way."

Sandra raised her head. Her eyes were glassy with tears, not yet ready to spill out.

"How much," she asked softly.

"I'm sorry, I can't hear you."

She raised her voice, "How much, I said, how much is the indemnity?"

The HR Director took a deep breath, this was the delicate part: "Five thousand euros."

"I've worked at the bank for twenty years, so that's two hundred and fifty euros for each year…"

"Well, if I may say, that's not the right way to look at it. You're not entitled to anything, so you can consider this a gift."

Sandra blinked, and the tears started to roll down her cheeks, she wiped them away with the back of her hand as they reached her jawline, then reached into a pocket, extracted a used tissue, and blew her nose. Cyril looked at her with disgust.

"Two hundred and fifty euros, is that all I'm worth?" She sobbed gently, rocking back and forth. A look of pity crossed the HR Director's face, and he opened his mouth to respond. But Cyril cut him off: "This is not a psychiatrist's office, Sandra, this is a bank, and banking is what we do, and that's *all* that we do."

Both men stood up, the meeting was over. "We'll conclude the transaction in my office," said the HR Director. After they left, Cyril de la Forêt du Maine opened wide the windows and reflected on how difficult his job could sometimes be.

#   #   #

Sandra walked home slowly, feeling the weight of the past weeks pushing from her head down to the soles of her feet. She showered, brushed her teeth, took a large Doliprane, and went to sleep. The next morning, she made an appointment to get her teeth cleaned, deposited the settlement check, and called Bruno. He said that he was helping Sauveur's cousins—some of whom were lawyers—to sort through his appointments. But he thought he'd be free to come to Lyon in a few days.

She set about the task of clearing out her apartment with newly found energy. The depression she had felt since last September had evaporated. She felt happy and light-headed, and she worked intensely, ditching old records, packing up most of her clothing to be given to charity. She boxed her books in sturdy cartons she picked up at a nearby Picard. She'd offer them to Bruno, but she doubted he'd take them, and she would look into giving them away as well.

Bruno appeared two days later. He was suntanned, but the skin around his eyes was pulled back into myriad creases, his cheeks looked hollow, and she wondered if he was getting enough sleep. Yet his face lit up when she said, "It went very well. Just like we thought it would."

"Did they ask you about your drinking?"

"Not a word. They just wanted to get rid of me as quickly as possible."

"Great. I see you've done a lot; let's finish getting you out of here."

#   #   #

Michel was wiping the bar sink clean when he looked up and saw Bruno in the doorway. "*Salut mec.*" He came around from behind the counter, put his hands on Bruno's arms, not quite an embrace, but as close as Michel could come to show affection.

"Coffee?" Bruno stirred the hot liquid, stared at the liquor bottles lined up on the wall behind the counter, looked for the right words. "It's my sister." A dull clink-clink, as Michel removed china cups and saucers from the dishwasher.

"Yeah, she's been through a rough patch, lost her job, and she's gone away to rest for a while." Clink-clink, Michel stacked the china next to the coffee machine. "I was wondering…" Michel looked up as if to ask what

194

was on the big man's mind, what was he getting at. "Yeah, we've had her mail forwarded to a post office box, and as I'm going to be traveling, I was wondering if you could check the box from time to time and hold any mail for me."

He was a strange one, Bruno was. What had he been doing in all those years since he'd left Lyon? Not a peep. Bruno had told him that he was working in Marseille, but now Bruno said he was going to be traveling. So, which was it? No point in asking questions, he'd just make up some story like the one about his sister.

"Sure, no problem. Glad to help."

Bruno reached into his pocket, removed a key, and placed it on the counter. "Thanks, *mec*." Michel tossed the key into a drawer in a small wooden tea chest. He would do as Bruno asked. He was curious when he'd see Bruno again, and what the story would be this time.

CHAPTER SIXTY-ONE

Neuilly-sur-Seine

THE DAYS WERE STARTING TO get longer, but winter wouldn't leave without a fight. The temperature dropped, daggers of cold striking down to the bones, and a tight gray lid of clouds seemed to have moved in for the duration. "I've got to get out of here," said Alex, "I'm going to go back to Trubenne. I'll feel closer to Charlotte there."

"Do you think that's a good idea?" asked Eugene. "I thought you didn't want to stay at Trubenne while Jacques was looking for you."

"Yeah," she replied, "I went to Marseille to be safe, and look how that turned out. Anyhow, it's not like I'm a celebrity, so how's he going to find me?"

Eugene didn't want to argue with Alex, but he planned to be away for a few days, and he didn't want to leave her alone in the deserted countryside. So, once at Trubenne, he would suggest spending only a few days there, before heading to Marseille, where he believed she would be safer. Of course, that meant that he'd have to share his plans with her. *I want to earn your trust,* he had once said, well, now was his chance.

Trubenne

Eugene went into the storage room where he'd left "Storm Over the Sea." He brought the painting into the kitchen where Alex was cooking. He wondered if she could feel Charlotte's presence, hear her voice, and imagine that they were chopping vegetables together, as they had done so many times.

"Where shall I put this, Madame?" he asked, the gold flecks dancing in his light brown eyes.

A pink flush crept up her neck, coming to rest just below her cheekbones: "Let's hang it in our bedroom, what do you think about that?"

That evening they built a fire in the massive chimney, just as they had done last fall, the comforting odor of burning wood filling the room. A bottle of Corbières was open, and Eugene poured them each a glass. There had been moments of tension between him and Alex; now all seemed calm and relaxed, but he was worried that warm mood might not last.

"I've been meaning to tell you, I'll be going away for a few days and I do think you'd be safer in Marseille than all alone at Trubenne."

"Oh, another mysterious project?" She smiled, and he could see that she tried to make her voice sound light, not accusing him of abandoning her, which was probably what she felt he was doing.

"Alex, listen to me, it's not what you think."

"I don't think anything. Life is too short to waste my time imagining what you're doing." Still smiling, she added, "If you don't trust me, so be it."

"I do trust you. Remember, I told you about how we think Mornnais has been collecting compromising information on the elites in France? My assignment was to meet him, negotiate his working with us, and failing that, to get his files. I got sidetracked trying to get my aunt's money back from him, but now that that's done, I need to finish what I started. I've learned that Jacques is at his château, and since I've made no headway with Bruno, the time has come for me to confront Jacques."

"Eugene, do you think that's realistic? I mean, why would he want to even see you, after you forced him to refund the money your aunt had paid for the fake Poussin."

"Of course, you're right. But you know the saying 'I'm going to make

Jacques an offer he can't refuse.'"

"And what might that be?"

"When I met Tony Perryman—remember, he's Thomas Smith's father—he gave me Tom's research notes. There's enough there to raise suspicions that Jacques is using *Artixia* as a front to steal artwork. While it may not be sufficient to make the charge stick in a court of law, Tom came up with enough dicey circumstances to smear Jacques' reputation."

"Aren't you worried what Jacques might do when cornered?"

"What worries me most is leaving you here at Trubenne."

In the morning, they drove to Charlotte's house in Marseille. Eugene spent the night there, and the next day he kissed Alex tenderly, got in his car, and headed north.

CHAPTER SIXTY-TWO

Marseille

SANDRA HAD LEFT THAT MORNING. For the time being, she would stay in a furnished studio that belonged to one of Bruno's acquaintances, melting into the noisy, colorful mass of humanity that was Marseille.

Bruno stayed behind to close Sandra's flat, quietly spreading the word that she was not well, that she had gone off for a long rest. He left Lyon on a blustery morning, the wind slowing him down as he rode his bike on the A7, heading to Marseille. As always, the weather changed after Valence, the gray clouds giving way to a luminous blue sky, the air warmer—the hazy mountains announcing that he was heading south. He found Sandra settling into her studio.

"Feeling better?"

"Much better, although I can't bring myself to drink a glass of wine."

"You're better off that way, take it from one who knows. How's this place? Is it okay?"

"Yes, no complaints. But how long will I be staying here?"

He couldn't help but notice how Sandra had aged. Was it the stress of the situation, the forced drinking, or was it just that inevitably imperceptible changes suddenly become apparent?

"Just lie low for a while until we're sure that you've been forgotten. I'll be checking your mail, see if anyone has tried to contact you, but from what you've told me, I think everyone at the bank was glad to see you gone."

"I guess. How did I ever wind up spending so much time with that bunch of assholes?"

"Don't think about it. Be happy that you're out of there, that's the best revenge."

"And what about you? Now that Sauveur is dead, are you going to stay on in Marseille?"

"For a while. Some of his associates asked me if I wanted to work for them, but once we've taken care of your situation, I'm out of here."

"And then what?"

Bruno's gaze rested on a point behind her head, a poster advertising the Friche Bel de Mai, all dark lines and bright colors.

"We'll see, I'm not sure. But right now, I've got to run an errand, I'll probably be away for a couple of days. I'll stop by to see you when I'm back."

They left the studio together, Bruno hopped back on his bike and Sandra decided to go for a walk. It felt strange to be free of obligations, to be at loose ends, to have extinguished her former life. A laugh started, deep in her belly, tears ran down her cheeks, washing over the network of fine red lines and into the corners of her mouth. *So, this is what it's like to feel happy.* A strange feeling, but Sandra would do her best to get used to it.

#   #   #

Bruno returned to his room on Rue Breteuil, packed up the few items he would need for his trip tomorrow. He walked down to Place aux Huiles, where he had an early dinner. He felt comfortable here in the wide-open space, bordered by graceful pastel Italianate buildings. Some tourists sat at two tables nearby. It was early in the season, but cruise ships docked in Marseille year-round these days. The tourists were Americans, and he was reminded of Eugene Stokes. He wondered where Stokes was, then his food came, and he gave all his attention to the plate of fried red snapper and black ink pasta. The waitress was a young Asian woman; for the first time since his accident, he felt a stirring in his loins, he had always gone for that type of girl. But Bruno had a long day ahead, and with some regret, he paid his bill and walked home. He was excited that his libido was returning, but even more excited that he would confront Jacques Mornnais in a few days.

CHAPTER SIXTY-THREE

Paris

JEAN-DANIEL BLANQUET FOLDED THE silk pocket square and carefully placed it in his jacket pocket. He had chosen a deep red with small white dots—he felt that it coordinated perfectly with his tie's red and blue stripes. It pained him that so many in his position—senior advisors—neglected to dress appropriately. He was small in stature, with a head of thick white hair, trimmed close. Short blunt bangs gave him a slightly monastic look. But he was more like a shark than a monk. Nicknamed *bonsai bis*, he was a special advisor to the President, another man of diminutive stature and killer instincts.

Seated behind a large Louis XV desk, leather-topped, gilt-trimmed mahogany, he stood up as his assistant ushered the visitors into his office. Kenneth Petit, tall and lanky, was a frequent visitor, as was the Prefect from the Bouches-du-Rhône. Jean-Daniel had been surprised to see Michel de Clermont d'Auvergne's name on the attendee list. Michel wore his aristocratic heritage casually, like an old vicuna coat. No need to flaunt it: that was for the *arrivistes*. Jean-Daniel always paid careful attention when he met Michel—he would be a valuable contact once he left the government.

The last man—with a deep tan and a shaved head— was unknown to him. He introduced himself: his name was Charles Paoli.

Kenneth Petit spoke first: "We believe that our friend has gone too far this time. Three deaths: the antique dealer Nicolas Pagès, *Maître* Paoli's cousin Sauveur Paoli, and Charlotte Vesla de Trubenne, a close family friend of Michel's. We cannot have thugs from Brezikstan running around murdering people, no matter how much uranium they sell us."

Jean-Daniel placed his elbows on the desk and put his hands together in an inverted V. He rested his chin on the apex, assuming a pensive posture. "Why did you say they were killed, our friend was selling fake paintings, is that it? And Mme Vesla de Trubenne, wrong place, wrong time, is that it?" he repeated, trying to keep the nervousness out of his voice. He continued, "We let him conduct his business as he sees fit, in exchange for services rendered. Very valuable services. I suppose I could have a word with him…" His voice drifted off.

Michel de Clermont d'Auvergne spoke: "I'm afraid it has gone far beyond that, Jean-Daniel. His thugs killed an innocent woman, and we cannot simply look the other way based on some misplaced notion of *raison d'état.* You need to accept responsibility for dealing with such an individual."

Jean-Daniel was not used to being reprimanded by anyone other than the President. Still, he tried to temporize: "I understand how you feel, Michel, but we're dealing with a very complicated situation."

Charles Paoli scowled, sat straight in his chair, his arms crossed on his chest: "In my opinion, it's not complicated at all. After my cousin realized that your man had sold him a forged painting, he asked for his money back. And for that, he was gunned down."

"Yes, of course, but please try to understand how inconvenient a trial would be. Accusations and wild rumors flying about, the only ones who would profit would be the press and the Opposition."

The Prefect shifted in his seat. He would have preferred to avoid a confrontation with the President's special advisor, but he felt under considerable pressure from the Paoli clan:

"That may well be, Jean-Daniel, but you need to remember that we have plenty of our own problems in Marseille, and this murder has not helped our reputation. Let your friend do as he likes in the Ile de France if you wish, but not in the Bouches-du-Rhône."

"Who said anything about a trial?" Kenneth Petit caught Charles Paoli's eye for a nano-second before the latter turned his head away.

"I hope you're not suggesting something extra-judicial."

"Of course not. I'm just suggesting that we take the time to have a serious talk with our friend."

The special advisor looked at the men, noticed for the first time that Charles Paoli had a crisp white pocket square. Classic, it went with the man's demeanor. He smiled, his lips pulled tightly across his teeth, "Well then, it's settled, isn't it? You'll have a talk with him, set him straight."

Jean-Daniel rose, signaling that the meeting was over. It had gone as they had expected, although he was pissed off at the way Michel had spoken to him. *Fucking aristocrat.* In any event, he felt that the President would be pleased.

Outside, the Prefect's car was waiting for him. The other three men walked towards the taxi stand; they shook hands as Charles Paoli got into a cab.

"Which way are you headed?" Kenneth Petit asked Michel.

"Oh, I think I'll walk a bit," he replied.

"Let's keep in touch," said Kenneth Petit as he too got into a cab and sped away.

#   #   #

Michel ruminated as he walked. *Bonsai bis,* the name filled his mouth with a metallic taste. He was used to people sucking up to him, thinking that he'd provide an entrée into a world otherwise beyond their reach. *Mistake.* When the little man was out of the Elysée Palace, he'd be of no interest to Michel. What had he said: *It's settled, you'll have a talk with him, set him straight.* They were afraid of Jacques spilling some of his secrets, fearful of disturbing the flow of uranium. And yet, they had realized that the Jacques was coming unhinged, and that too was a danger. He imagined he knew what *setting him straight* meant. It was not the outcome he would have preferred, but when the State was involved.... He turned on to Rue Boissy d'Anglas, breathed a sigh of satisfaction as he rang the bell at the sculpted wooden doors and entered the comfort of a place that was like a second home.

CHAPTER SIXTY-FOUR

Château d'Hélène

CHARLES-ANTOINE HAD RETURNED FROM his morning errand: picking up the daily newspapers that Jacques perused with particular interest. He stood at the door to Jacques's office, parcel in hand. "Good morning, sir."

Seeing his chauffeur, Jacques again regretted Tarek's passing. The new man—could he still be called a new man after all these months—was so stiff, so formal. No doubt Charles-Antoine's previous employers had expected him to act that way. But Jacques had preferred Tarek's nonchalance, the barely hidden sneer, even if he had been fucking his wife. He considered that a sign of Tarek's good taste, it was Mila who had disappointed him.

"Ah, Charles-Antoine, good morning." Charles-Antoine placed the newspapers on Jacques' desk.

"Sir, the Check Engine light is on. I need to take the car into the garage."

"Yes, you'd best take care of that right away."

Charles-Antoine called the garage and asked if he could bring the car in tomorrow morning. He'd leave it there all day if that were okay with them. The garage was very busy, but as it was Mr. Mornnais, they would manage. Later in the day, Charles-Antoine knocked on Jacques' door again. "Yes?"

"Sir, I managed to get an appointment for tomorrow morning. And Sir, Mercie has asked if she can come into town with me to do some shopping. It shouldn't take too long."

Do I give a fuck about Mercie's shopping? Had she been alive, Charles-Antoine would have gone to Mila. Instead, here he was bothering him. "Yes, of course." He picked up his cellphone, signaling that the discussion was over.

#   #   #

The driver and Mercie were on their way into town. Jacques paced in circles, telephone glued to his ear. On his third time around, he brushed against a worktable, his eye drawn to a pile of magazines that had accumulated over the past month. He had made it a practice to scour the popular press for any nugget of information that he could use. It was time to catch-up. As soon as his call ended, he sat down and started to leaf through the magazines. With lips pursed in frustration—nothing of interest caught his attention—he threw the useless magazines on the floor. There remained a last issue, one of those publications that chronicled the lives of royalty and members of the aristocracy. *Do people read this shit to add a dash of color to their otherwise dull lives?* He frowned until he came across a story about the tragic death of a member of one of France's oldest families: Charlotte Vesla de Trubenne. Jacques was very familiar with the events that led to Charlotte's death and that of her companion, Sauveur Paoli. He knew, too, that Charlotte's niece, Alexia Thornhill, had been injured in the attack. His eyes traveled down the article and stopped at the photos of Charlotte and her niece. Jacques' pulse quickened and his frown became a smirk as he recognized Alexia Thornhill: he was looking at the woman who had sat next to him on the flight to Paris, the woman who had called herself Nathalie Martin

Reading further, he learned that Alexia Thornhill was the great-niece of Richard Vesla de Trubenne. It wouldn't be very difficult to find her, discover what Tony Perryman's son had told her, as well as anything else she might know.

What a great day it was turning out to be. He thought again of how easy it had been to rob Renaud Schneider's gallery. A pity that the man might be peddling fakes, but he knew that he'd find a way around that. And, of course, he now had a state-of-the-art swimming pool. An inaugural swim was long overdue. As soon as he finished his swim, he would arrange to find and question Alexia Thornhill.

He went up to his bedroom and changed into his swimming trunks. He averted his gaze from the full-length mirror. There was nothing there that he needed to see. He had never been much for sports, never walked when he could be driven, his body a mute testimony to the consequences of an inactive lifestyle. No, one could not count six-pack abs, sculpted shoulders, or muscular legs among his considerable achievements. *I've done a lot more than that,* he thought, as he went down the stairway to his pool.

CHAPTER SIXTY-FIVE

Château d'Hélène

THE THREE MEN PARKED UNDER the trees that lined the drive leading to the château. The van was not new: "Manual Diaz Décoration & Renovation," a phone number, and an email address, were stenciled in black on the dirty, scratched white surface.

They peered cautiously through the large windows, before letting themselves into the house. Silence. They knew that the driver and the maid were gone, not due back for several hours, but where was Jacques? The reception rooms, his office, the dining rooms, and the kitchen: all empty. They broke the lock on the door to the library—he was not there either. They noticed that the entrance to the cellar was open. One of the men remained in the entry while the other two crept softly down the stairs, continued past the wine cave, and came to the pool. A man was slowly swimming the breaststroke. When he reached one end, he'd hang on the side for a moment, and then swim another length.

The two men exchanged glances, "wait," the leader gestured. They watched as Jacques stopped midway to catch his breath, swam to the ladder, climbed out of the pool, and wrapped a thick robe around his body. The cold air hit him as he opened the poolroom door. An intake of breath, eyes squeezed closed. When he opened them, the first thing that he saw were two sets of brown eyes, one full mouth, the other almost lipless, the rest of their faces hidden by balaclavas. One of the men pushed him to the ground, and with his knee in Jacques's back, he bound his hands with a pair of flex cuffs.

"What the fuck?"

"Stay calm," said the full mouth, "We won't hurt you if you behave yourself." He pulled Jacques to his feet.

"Do you know who I am?"

"Yes, we do, that's why we're here." The words frightened him; a warm trickle ran down his leg.

"Now look what you've done," said the lipless one, and they both laughed.

"Get the van," shouted the full mouth, as they marched Jacques up the stairs. His mind raced with possibilities: the Brezikstanis, the French, a couple of thugs for hire….

"Who sent you," his voice firm, anger overcoming his fear.

"All in good time, my friend, all in good time."

Jacques felt a stinging in his forearm; before he lost consciousness, he knew what it was. He had, after all, used the same tactic on more than one occasion. The van had pulled up to the front of the château. The driver spread an antique kilim on the polished parquet floor. They placed Jacques on the rug, rolled it up around him, and tied it neatly in place.

The rug joined the other objects in the van: parts of chairs, an old gilt mirror, lengths of brocade, and tattered lace. They drove slowly down the drive, and when they reached the road, headed towards the highway.

CHAPTER SIXTY-SIX

Château d'Hélène

BRUNO STOOD OUTSIDE A STONE cottage at the river's edge. He hadn't been back since that time last year when he'd crawled up the riverbank, more dead than alive. Bruno had lost his memory in the freezing river, but now it had returned. Not only that, but new thoughts, things that he hadn't wanted to remember, had intruded on his consciousness. A fleeting temptation: jump back into the river and try to lose those thoughts again. The problem was, first, he wasn't sure it would work, and second, he didn't want to forget *everything*, just certain things.

He glanced at the château in the distance, turned, found the key to the cottage in its hiding place, and unlocked the door. Inside, all was as he had left it: the rumpled bed, the food wrappers, and the decrepit furnishings. A rat scurried out from under the old buffet, it startled him, and then he laughed, *yeah, there are a lot of rats around here.*

Bruno hoped that he'd find Jacques at home, but if not, he'd brought food and would hide out in the cottage until Jacques appeared. Then he could complete some of the unfinished images that rattled his brain, ricocheting, getting tangled up in each other.

\#   \#   \#

Eugene had plenty of time to think during the drive from Marseille to Château d'Hélène. He took secondary roads, bypassing the major highways; he preferred to avoid being photographed each time he paid a toll. The promise of spring hung in the soft air; fluffy white clouds floated in the sky like small cotton balls.

Eugene had called Jacques. "I have a business proposition for you. I hope there are no hard feelings about our last transaction, but I think you would have acted the same way, had you been in my shoes."

When he heard Eugene's voice, Jacques's first impulse had been to hang up, but curiosity got the best of him. They had agreed to meet two days later at Château d'Hélène. Eugene would have preferred someplace more public, but he was anxious to have the meeting: the time had come to act. He felt the familiar tingle of excitement at the back of his neck.

He'd told Alex that he would make Jacques an offer he couldn't refuse, but was that so? He imagined sitting across from Jacques, making his pitch. *Your files in exchange for your reputation. What if he doesn't nibble? No what-ifs. He will.* He braked sharply as a squirrel dashed in front of the car. For the remainder of the trip, he focused on the road.

It was dusk, the brilliant sun was falling towards the horizon, and for the first time, he noticed the neat hedges, the geometric fields, and the graceful trees on the ridge of a hill. *It's not like Trubenne, but it's beautiful, nonetheless.* The fatigue of the long trip set in, and he stopped to spend the night in a two-star hotel in a town so ugly it reminded him of a blemish on a pretty girl's face. The bed was lumpy, the wallpaper faded and starting to peel away at the seams; the linoleum floor was streaked in places where the color had worn away. Early the next morning, the owner—*she must be the owner*, he doubted that the hotel could afford to pay anyone to work there—was mopping down the entrance. With the acrid smell of ammonia burning his nostrils, he settled the bill, found the town's one open café, and breakfasted on acidic coffee and a stale croissant. If Eugene cared about such things, he would have concluded that it was not an auspicious beginning. However, it made no difference to him.

It was just after midday when he passed a white van traveling in the opposite direction. He turned off the road and onto the long drive that led to Chateau d'Hélène.

CHAPTER SIXTY-SEVEN

Château d'Hélène

JACQUES WALKED TOWARDS HIM, HOLDING an envelope in his hand; he hurried to meet him, but the distance between them remained the same. He lunged forward, trying to close the gap, his hand outstretched to grab the envelope. Jacques disappeared, replaced by a thin figure in a long black robe, its face in a shadow; it too had an outstretched hand. "Viens, mon petit," said the apparition. He found that odd, for he knew that he was a grown man. This time, the gap closed, the shadow faded. "Mon Père," he replied.

The cottage had the smell of the river, rank, and cold. It had the stench of body odor, of fear, of anger and frustration. Bruno shivered in the damp, fetid air, stripped off his sweat-soaked clothes, put on dry garments, and stepped outside. Once again, he had slept poorly. He had come to dread the moment when he closed his eyes; he never knew when the nightmares would return. A cool breeze blew off the river. Staring at the reeds, he took a deep breath: *I'm going to put an end to this, starting right now.*

Bruno walked along the riverbank towards the big house, keeping his eyes open for any sign of activity. He stopped at the shipping containers where the painters had worked. Hadn't the American said that they had left? But Bruno wondered if anyone had replaced them. He pushed the door open and stepped inside. The room was empty: no furniture, none of the paints and brushes and bottles that Li and Wen had used. Someone had even scrubbed the place clean. It looked like Jacques had made other arrangements, as far as the painters were concerned. *Where had the painters gone?*

Bruno left the shipping containers and as he approached the château, he pushed the painters to the back of his mind and focused on finding Jacques. He stood outside the kitchen, stuck his head up against the barred window: the room was empty. *Where was the maid?* He walked around to the front; the car was not there. The man who had replaced Tarek—where was he? Driving Jacques, taking the maid shopping, running an errand? He wondered if Jacques was even there and if he was alone. The drapes had been pulled back, and he tried to look through a crack in the gauzy white curtains to get a glimpse inside. Nothing. He walked around the château, looking through windows where he could, but he saw no one, heard no voices. Could Jacques be away in Paris, in Singapore, or in Brezikstan? Seriously pissed off, he returned to the front door. Had he really come all this way for nothing? How long was he going to hang out in that fuck-awful cottage? Fueled by rage and frustration, he grabbed one of the brass knockers on the front door, ready to pound it, and tripped as the door opened.

\#   \#   \#

"Not too steady on our feet, are we?"

Bruno jumped up, ready to fight; he froze as he recognized the man he knew as Eugene Stokes. "What the fuck?"

"I was about to make the same observation, my dear friend Bruno. What the fuck are *you* doing here?"

Bruno sneered, "It's obvious isn't it, I've come to visit Jacques, I guess you have too. But we're out of luck, he's not at home."

Eugene could sense that Bruno was nervous, on edge. *It wouldn't surprise me if he's come to kill Jacques; I need to hold him off long enough to talk to Jacques first.* "Since the door's open, why don't we look inside?

You never know what we might find."

They wiped their feet on the door-mat—old habits die hard—and Eugene followed Bruno up to the second floor, where paint chips from the faded beige walls littered the floor. Bruno went to Ella's room, pulled a small suitcase out from under the bed, and read the name on the luggage tag: Mercedes Almodiel. He fingered the cheap polyester garments hanging on a wire in the armoire: "These are too big for Ella," he said, "it looks like she's been replaced."

"Oh, didn't I tell you, she's back in the Philippines."

"No, you didn't tell me. Don't you think I would remember that?"

"Well, anyway, now you know, so let's get on with it."

They went down to the first floor, where the moldings and walls were freshly painted, the parquet floor waxed to a warm patina. Bruno went first to his old room. It had been cleaned out, the bed stripped, the closet and drawers were empty, all trace of his presence removed. He was not surprised, yet it irritated him to see how completely his existence had been erased. It was evident that another man was now living in Tarek's room, again, no surprises there. The guest rooms were unoccupied, which just left Jacques's bedroom. The door was ajar. Pants, a jacket, and a shirt had been tossed carelessly on the bed. Underwear and socks were strewn on the floor near a pair of shoes.

"Looks like he changed clothes before going out."

"Strange that he would change his underwear, did he have some kind of obsession with clean boxers?"

Bruno shrugged, "Who gives a flying fuck? Let's go downstairs."

"Hold on a minute there, I want to take a closer look." Eugene poked around the bedroom, opening drawers, looking through the clothing hanging in the walk-in closet.

"There's nothing here," he said before he stopped to look in a wastepaper basket. He lifted a plastic bag, and clothing tags marked *Vilebrequin*. "He's got better taste in bathing trunks than in his suits, that's for sure. Looks like our friend has gone out for a swim."

"Jacques swimming? Don't make me laugh. His only exercise was getting in and out of the Merc. Let's check the office, that's bound to be more interesting."

They descended the imposing central staircase. Mila had liked to compare it to the one at the Opéra de Paris. It was indeed grand, but that was pushing the envelope clean off the table. Bruno ran down the steps rapidly, Eugene took his time, surveying the entrance hall. "What's that?" he pointed to a sliver of light that outlined a partially open door.

"Oh, nothing. That's the door to the cellar, do you suppose Jacques went down there this morning to get himself a bottle of wine?

"I don't suppose anything, so I'd like to take a look. I always wanted to visit a rich man's wine cellar. "

This time it was Eugene who led the way. At the bottom of the stairs, the air was dank. Lining the wall were hundreds of bottles; many were coated in dust and cobwebs. He stopped and sniffed. Mixed in the cold, damp air was something that smelled like chlorine.

Eugene continued walking, with Bruno behind him, and came to a halt at the open door to the pool space. "Well, I'll be damned, he built a fucking pool down here. I thought you said he wasn't into exercise very much."

"This is news to me. Jacques must have built the pool after I was gone."

Eugene touched Bruno's arm gently: "If you don't mind, stay here. I want to go inside the enclosure, one person is enough, we don't want to mess things up."

He slipped off his shoes, and walked gingerly to the edge of the pool, saw that it was empty. He circled the pool's perimeter, following the trail of drops of water that started at the ladder and led to the poolroom door. Before, he hadn't paid attention to the corridor that led to the pool. Now, he got down on his knees and thought he could make out two sets of footprints; if there had been visitors to the cellar, they hadn't bothered to wipe the dirt off their shoes.

"I can't be sure, but I think our friend met up with some company, and they all left together. Strange that he didn't bother to get dressed."

"It looks like someone got to him before us. *Merde*."

They were back in the entryway. "So, what are you going to do now?" asked Eugene.

"Get what I came for."

"What's that?"

"Back wages."

"And where might they be?"

"I'm trying to remember. Shut the fuck up, would you?"

Eugene followed Bruno as he went to Jacques' office, sat down in the chair facing his desk, and closed his eyes. Suddenly they popped open: "And you never did say what you were doing here."

"I came to make him a business proposition. The guy was a shit magnet, and I was going to make him an irresistible offer."

Bruno again closed his eyes. He came into the office as Jacques bent down to lift a box filled with files. Ah, Bruno, give me a hand with this. What is it, Jacques? It's part of my multi-risk insurance policy, he laughed. They walked to the library. Jacques unlocked the door and took the box from Bruno's hands. Okay, you can go now. Bruno turned to leave, stopped, and stood with his back to the outer wall, watching Jacques through the partly opened door. Saw him slide the bookcase to one side. He turned and padded noiselessly down the carpeted hallway and returned to the office to wait for Jacques.

"I think I've got it." He removed a knife from his pocket, used it to pry open the top drawer of Jacques' desk, and removed a set of keys on a ring. Oblivious to the other man's presence, he strode rapidly to the library, only to find the lock was broken and the door ajar. He again saw Jacques standing in front of the bookshelves, and he took his place, laid his hands in the same spot. He pressed gently; Jacques was not a powerful man, there was no need for excessive force. Bruno felt the inner latch come undone and slowly slid the bookcase to one side. *Putain* he hissed, *putain*. Eugene stood with his back to the shuttered window, looked beyond Bruno's shoulder to the two exposed bookcases. He took in neat piles of currency stacked on the shelves of one bookcase, and boxes of files in the other.

"Looks like you found what you came for." Eugene's voice jolted Bruno.

"You bet," Bruno replied as he reached for a pile of black carrier bags at the bottom of the bookcase and started to empty the contents of the shelves into two of them.

"Mind if I have a look here," asked Eugene.

Bruno seemed to be orbiting another planet, one with an endless supply of cash, and Eugene didn't want to draw his attention to the second bookcase. "Yeah, whatever." He continued to stuff the bags with cash.

Eugene counted thirteen boxes: there were eleven full boxes for each year from 2000 to 2010; another box dated 2011 with a few files. His heart skipped a beat when he saw the last box: it was labeled "Ukraine."

CHAPTER SIXTY-EIGHT

Château d'Hélène

IT WAS NOT UNTIL LATER in the afternoon that the garage had checked all the Mercedes' systems. A few minor unnecessary parts were changed, an invoice issued for the account of Mr. Jacques Mornnais. He was an excellent client, and they would not ask the driver to pay the bill immediately. Charles-Antoine had given Mercie two fifty Euro bills. He'd had a lucky night playing cards, and he said it brought good luck to share your good fortune. Mercie bought a scarf that was on sale; she kept the rest of the money because you never knew when your luck would run out.

Dusk was falling by the time they arrived back at the château. Bruno had turned the alarm system on before leaving, so it took some time for the fire department to come and open the door. It took some more time for Charles-Antoine and Mercie to help the Gendarmes search the house and for them to conclude that Jacques was missing.

Charles-Antoine and Mercie spent the night at the château. The next day, they drove to Paris, and Charles-Antoine left the car in the parking garage on Rue du Vieux-Colombier. They both suspected that Jacques Mornnais would not require their services in the future. The following week, Charles-Antoine started a new job, and his employer found Mercie a job taking care of two small children in the sixteenth arrondissement.

\#   \#   \#

Bruno and Eugene threw the carrier bags onto the back floor of Eugene's car. They placed the boxes in the trunk and on the back seat. Bruno returned to the cottage, packed up his affairs, and rolled the motorcycle down the bank and into the river. He placed the padlock on the door and put the key back in its hiding place. He had no intention of returning, but you never knew.

"What do you think happened to Jacques," Eugene asked.

Bruno stared at the road ahead, "I don't think he's dead. I mean, whoever they are, they could have killed him and just left him there."

"Well, at least you got your back wages, and then some."

"Yeah, but I had a few things to say to Jacques, and you tell me that bitch is back in the Philippines, and I had a few things to say to her as well. It's not over 'til it's over."

Eugene had an inkling of what "say a few things" meant but saw no point in continuing that conversation. "Do you mind some classical music?"

"Whatever."

Eugene slipped a CD of Arthur Rubenstein playing Chopin's Nocturnes into the deck. It was incredible how you could hear every note, feel the passion, the compositions like perfect pieces of crystal. He recalled a paperweight on Richard's desk at Trubenne. It was an imperfect piece of crystal, the colors irregular, alternating between bright and cloudy. Damaged goods, not unlike Bruno. The man was complicated, intelligent, sometimes thuggish, and with a barely controlled penchant for violence; yet Eugene sensed a streak of fragility in that tough frame. Perhaps he'd had an unhappy childhood? Maybe so, but that didn't necessarily turn you into a sociopath.

His last thought, as he dropped him off in front of the train station in Dijon, was whether Bruno had remembered more than he had lost, and he felt uneasy thinking about what that might mean. But he consoled himself; it was doubtful that he would ever see Bruno again. He hoped not.

221

CHAPTER SIXTY-NINE

Dijon

BRUNO SAT ON A SIDEWALK bench, watched Eugene drive away, and waited. When he was sure that the American was not returning, he walked to a nearby hotel. It was inexpensive and clean, large enough to provide some anonymity —he'd been there before. The copies of lithographs of Dijon monuments on the pastel walls, a geometric patterned bedspread, the tiny desk with its leatherette covered brochure: it was all vaguely familiar but brought back no memories.

He stretched out on the bed and closed his eyes, visualized the last time he was in the hotel. He was in his room—it was not that different from this one—and he had felt comfortable there. Bruno had been sitting at the tiny desk; he had looked at his phone and started to punch the keypad. Loud voices echoed in the corridor outside his room. A family was preparing to visit Dijon's historical center, the children excited to be in a foreign country, the parents trying to calm them down. The image faded, and he opened his eyes. *Merde.*

It had been several days since he'd bathed, and he went into the white-tiled bathroom and turned on the shower. He forgot about Jacques Mornnais, the painters, the maid Ella, and his dreams, savored the feel of the pulsating hot water running over his body. At last, he stepped out of the shower. As if in one of his dreams, he traced a phone number in the mist on the mirror. His hand moved again, and he wrote "Laurent."

Putain, that's it. He'd dealt with Laurent before. Jacques had used him when he needed to transfer cash abroad. Now he saw him quite clearly; a skinny guy, he looked like some nerdy accountant. Everything about him was black: the frames of the thick glasses perched on a pointy nose, his hair, his three-day beard, his deep-set eyes, two small orbs that locked on to you like a laser.

Laurent showed up in the late afternoon. For no reason, he laughed nervously as Bruno dumped the contents of the two carrier bags on the patterned bedspread. The five hundred Euro notes looked like lumps of shit. The French franc notes had been so beautiful, the fucking European bureaucrats couldn't get anything right, not even the color of money. Whatever. They counted the packets: fifty bills to a pack, one hundred little packages, two and a half million Euros. The money was a small consolation for having missed Jacques, but hey, he'd taken what he could get.

The transaction didn't take long. They agreed on Laurent's commission — hefty, but he was not in a position to argue. A transfer for the balance was done to Bruno's account in Singapore. After that, the non-descript, mousy-looking little man left the hotel room, pulling a battered wheeled suitcase behind him.

Bruno didn't know for whom Laurent worked: he was nothing more than an errand boy. Perhaps his boss would call Jacques? He chuckled; he was sure that the call would go unanswered, and that Jacques had more important shit on his plate if he was even still alive. After dinner— his first proper meal in days—he wandered through the historic center. In the old days, he would have spent the night in his favorite clubs, but like so many who had kicked booze, he could no longer stand to be in the company of heavy drinkers.

It had been a long day, a lot had happened since he had awakened this morning, wrapped in a smelly blanket in a filthy bed in the stone cottage. He showered again; this time, no new thoughts came up to the surface, and he slipped between the sheets, hoping for a dreamless sleep.

CHAPTER SEVENTY

Marseille

ALEX FOLDED HER COUSIN'S CLOTHING carefully, as though she was touching Charlotte herself. By mid-afternoon, she had finished placing the garments in gray bin liners, and she called Emmaus to come and pick them up. Alex was sure Charlotte would have wanted to help those in need. But she held back an old black cloche that Charlotte put on all the time, not to wear but as a reminder of her loss. The effort to let go left her feeling exhausted, empty.

Eugene had called to say that he'd be back that evening. Too tired to cook, she dragged herself out to buy a roast chicken and potatoes. At the bakery, she bought a baguette and some fruit tarts. She couldn't be bothered to figure out what they would eat the next day; tomorrow would take care of itself in due course.

Alex was at the front door— *shit, what have I done with my keys?* She dumped her purchases on the ground, and as she rummaged in her purse, she was unaware of the man coming up behind her.

"Madame Thornhill?" Startled, she dropped her keys, and turned to see sunglasses perched on a round shaven head; it was the color of dark honey. The man wore an expensive overcoat, his shoes were polished, and he smiled as he spoke: "I'm sorry, I didn't mean to frighten you. You *are* Alexia Thornhill?"

"Yes, and you are…"

"Forgive me, my name is Charles Paoli, I'm a cousin of Sauveur Paoli."

He spoke with a heavy accent; his voice was warm, and his face reminded her of Sauveur.

She picked up her keys. "I am so sorry for your loss," he continued.

"Thank you. So am I for your loss."

Should I invite him in? The place is such a mess…." He interrupted her thoughts: "I do not want to disturb you, Madame Thornhill, but if I can ever be of help, please do not hesitate to call on me." He handed her his card, held her hand for a moment in his two hands, bowed his head, and walked away.

Night had fallen by the time Eugene returned. Driving around the narrow, hilly streets, looking for a place to park, he wondered if he was condemned to drive until dawn when he saw an empty space right in front of the house. Alex had been on the lookout for him: the front door opened, she ran out, threw her arms around his neck.

"I'm so glad you're back."

"Me too," he nuzzled her neck, kissed her tenderly.

"I just need to take care of one or two things."

She dropped her arms, "Okay," and took a step back.

"It won't take long, I promise."

Eugene went back to the car, took out the box marked 'Ukraine,' and carried it into the house. "I just need to arrange for someone to pick up some stuff I have in the car."

"Are you running guns or selling dope?" She tried to smile, pretend she was joking, to hide her irritation. She felt that once again, Eugene was shutting her out of a part of his life.

"No," he laughed, "it's nothing like that. Just paper. If you don't believe me, come and see for yourself." He took her by the hand, led her to the car and opened the back door so that she could see the boxes.

"If you wish, I'll open any one you want."

"No, I'm good," and she walked back into the house.

CHAPTER SEVENTY-ONE

Washington, DC

HE HAD EATEN A PASTRAMI on rye, extra pickle, finished a large Diet Coke. A belch of satisfaction was making its way out of his stomach when his phone rang. He let go with a second belch and picked up the receiver.

"Mmyes?"

"It's me, I got the stuff we talked about. You'll need to send someone to pick it up right now."

"What's your address?" He wrote it down, "Okay, give me a half an hour. I'll call you back. And Gene, well done."

Another fucking asshole who thinks I need a nickname. "Thanks, make it quick, I'm hungry and tired."

A black van with Bouches-du-Rhône license plates left the parking space in front of the US Consulate on the little Place Varian Fry and drove to Vauban. It pulled up next to Eugene's car—two men got out and loaded twelve boxes into the van. Seven hours later, the van drove into the courtyard of the US embassy in Paris. Jacques Mornnais might have been called away on urgent business, but his files would take on a life of their own.

\# # #

Marseille

They ate the roast chicken and potatoes, bathed in the rotisserie's special sauce. The wine was an undistinguished Bordeaux, but they were too tired to care. Eugene took in the dark circles under Alex's eyes, her face all in angles, the pale skin pulled tightly across her cheekbones. She had never looked more beautiful to him. He felt a warmth spread through his chest; how lucky he was to have met a woman like Alex, how close he had come to losing her. Her arm was resting on the table; he reached across and put his hand on hers.

Eugene remembered the day of their reconciliation in Café Carré and saw himself telling her that he'd tell her everything. And he had told her everything—about why he was chasing after Jacques Mornnais. Still, he'd held back; there were other secrets he'd kept to himself. But now, once he'd looked at the Ukraine file, he'd find the right moment to share his deepest thoughts and desires with Alex.

EPILOGUE

CAROLINE WAS BACK AT HER job. The bookstore was air-conditioned, and when she stepped outside, she felt enveloped by a hot, moist blanket. Aside from the drama that had surrounded her trip to Marseille, the cooler air had been a welcome change from Phuket's tropical climate. *Will I ever get used to this* she wondered, rivulets of perspiration running down her back. At day's end, she went to an internet café to check her mail; she had opened an email account so that she could stay in touch with Patrick.

The windows were open to let in any stray breeze, but the room was sweltering. This won't take more than a minute, Caroline thought. Patrick's message was short: could she send five hundred Euros to tide him over until he started a new job? She shook her head and typed a quick response: Thanks for asking about me, oh, you didn't, sorry. I'll see what I can do. *I'm halfway around the world, and nothing has changed.*

The following morning, there was a knock on the door to her cubicle at the back of the shop: "Excuse me, I was wondering if you could help me?" That voice. She looked up to see Sandra Picardeau's form filling the doorway: "What are you doing here?" Caroline's voice was subdued, her mouth set in a hard line to match her angry eyes.

"Now Caroline, is that any way to greet an old friend? You ought to show a little more gratitude."

"And what's that supposed to mean?"

"Did you really think that I *forgot* to lock my desk drawer? How many times did I run out of the office, leaving it open? I thought you'd *never* catch on."

"You mean…"

"Yes, I mean, I *facilitated* your little operation. So, half of the money was rightfully mine, and you don't need to put on such a long face. Lucky for me, my brother showed up and was able to find you."

"You've got your money, so why are you here?"

"I just wanted to be sure that you *understood*. If it weren't for me, you'd still be sitting in front of your computer in that dreary bank, doing your dreary, meaningless job."

Caroline sat like a piece of brown, petrified wood, reliving the moment when Sandra had rushed out of the office to bring Bruno to the hospital. "That's a load of bullshit. I think you forgot to lock your desk, and now you're trying to make it seem as though you did me a *favor.*"

"Think whatever you like. I'm leaving in the morning, and I thought I'd buy you a drink. I doubt that we'll see each other again."

"Thanks for the invitation, but I think I'll pass."

"As you wish, Caroline. Although I must say, I don't see why you picked this impossibly humid place, overrun by sex tourists and backpackers, when you had the whole world to choose from." At that moment, Caroline was asking herself the same question.

#   #   #

Phyllis Peters opened a package of Scottish shortbread cookies, arranged them on a glass plate, and set the plate on the table between two unmatched mugs. She stood at the window, watching the raindrops slide down the panes and kept an eye out for Sylvia. A form appeared, a black mushroom making its way to her building. Phyllis moved across the room to the intercom, stood, waiting for Sylvia to ring the bell, and when she did, buzzed her in. Sylvia peeled off her raincoat and rain hat, revealing several layers of gray and black polyester, trimmed in gray and white lace. She removed her red plastic boots and padded over to the table.

"Tea? Is Earl Gray okay?" asked Phyllis. Without waiting for an answer, she went into the kitchen, hung three teabags on the side of the teapot and boiled water. When the tea was ready, she brought the pot into the living room and sat down at the table, facing Sylvia.

"I haven't seen much of you lately; you must be quite busy settling your brother's estate." Perhaps Sylvia should have gone more slowly, talked about the lousy weather, said how much she adored Scottish shortbread. But as is too often the case, avarice trumped good manners.

Phyllis smiled, an enigmatic pursing of the lips, "Oh yes," and sighed.

"So, how are things going, with the apartment and the house and the paintings?"

"Oh, I've put the apartment on the market." Sylvia's face fell into a mask of disappointment. "I think I already told you I was going to do that. Would you like some tea? Have a cookie, they're delicious."

Sylvia took her time, sipped the hot tea slowly. "So, you're going to live in that cold, damp house in the country?"

"Now Sylvia, it's very well heated, as you know. And yes, I'm going to spend some time there, surrounded by beautiful paintings. I'm sure Merv would have liked that idea."

"You're not going to put any of them up for sale? "

Phyllis stirred her tea, choosing her words, moving the polyester princess into place.

"The situation has changed somewhat."

"Oh, really?"

"Yes. You remember our meeting with Mr. Denton, the executor? He said that we needed an appraisal of the paintings. In February, he called me to say that the man who was doing the appraisal needed information on the provenance of the paintings, and he was wondering if I could help. Now, in fact, I do have some papers that Merv left with me, but I haven't shared that information with Mr. Denton.

"I don't think I'm following you, Phyllis."

A fleeting smirk animated Phyllis' placid features before she resumed control of her emotions. "Sylvia, let me draw you a picture. My brother had an art consultant, a man named Jack Mornaize, who introduced him to an art dealer. His name was Nicolas Pages. When Mr. Denton told me that the expert was not certain that Merv's paintings were originals, I called M. Pages, the man who sold him the paintings. I learned that he was deceased and that his daughter didn't have any of his business records. Then I called the consultant, Mr. Mornaize, to see if he could help with establishing the provenance. Are you following me, Sylvia?"

Sylvia nodded, "Yes, I am."

"It wasn't easy to get to talk to Mr. Mornaize; I had to leave several messages, but eventually, he called me back. He said that he had no information on the chain of ownership, other than what Mr. Pages had already provided to Merv. He was sorry he couldn't help me further. I felt he was brushing me off, I mean, how could he know so little if he was Merv's consultant? I tried to reach him again, but the phone just rang until the line cut. Then I called Mr. Denton and asked if he could help me to contact Mr. Mornaize, but he said he'd never heard of him."

"But you said you have some papers your brother left; why don't you provide those to the expert?"

"Because I think there's something fishy about them. I've been asking myself why Merv sent them to me to put in a safe deposit box? What was he worried about? And remember how on edge he was when he visited in December?"

"I hadn't noticed, but if you say so… I don't know, Phyllis, would you like me to look at your brother's papers? I mean, maybe I could tell you what I think." Phyllis smiled inwardly. She suspected that Sylvia was trying to sound tentative, not really that interested, but the schoolteacher was satisfied that she'd moved her friend into place for the next steps.

"Really, you wouldn't mind?"

"No, I'm glad to be of help."

Phyllis rose, walked over to the carved wooden buffet, removed Merv's files, and placed them on the table. "Your tea must be cold; can I get you another cup?" She went into the kitchen to boil water and left Sylvia to look through the files.

\#   \#   \#

Sylvia closed the last file, brought the cup to her lips, but the tea had gone cold again. Not that it mattered. "I see what you meant when you said you didn't see the point of sharing these files with the expert. They'll only confirm his suspicions. You did well to say nothing about them."

"Well, at least I'll pay fewer taxes. And some of the paintings are quite beautiful, and I think I'll bring them out to the house in Normandy."

"When you think about it, there's so little separating an original from a fake."

"Do you believe that, Sylvia?"

"Oh, yes, quite. For example, you said your brother loved his collection. He called it his secret garden. What made him change his mind? Just some words on a piece of paper."

"I guess that's one way of looking at it."

"Perhaps I could do some research, help to strengthen the chain of ownership for certain paintings…After that, I might find suitable buyers for you, what do you think?"

It had taken a few hours and several pots of tea. Still, without any urging, Phyllis had gotten Sylvia to offer to continue the work started by Nicolas Pagès and Jacques Mornnais. And she hadn't shed a single tear.

\#   \#   \#

Richard awoke long before daybreak; he'd been an early riser since childhood, eager to see what the day held in store for him. He showered and dressed, slipped on a cashmere jacket, but decided that he couldn't be bothered to wear a tie—that was one of the benefits of retirement. Richard had the feeling that he'd forgotten something, a thought lurking just outside the edge of memory. Was this happening more frequently, he asked himself, or was it just that he'd had so much more to remember as of late? He was having breakfast when Maria came in to announce that his nephew Vital had arrived. *Merde,* he thought, *I'd forgotten that he was coming this morning.* "Of course, ask him to come in."

Vital Vesla de Trubenne, VeeVee to both those who wished him well and those who did not, walked into the kitchen. Some people carry their own cloud of joy, or sorrow, depression, or happiness. They walk into a room, and the atmosphere gets brighter or dimmer. When VeeVee walked into a room, it was never without an agenda, and the atmosphere stiffened to ward off whatever he was pitching.

"*Bonjour,* Richard," he bent to move his lips in the vicinity of his uncle's forehead, and formalities terminated, sat down facing him.

"*Bonjour,* Vital." Richard's eyeballs were ringed with red, the purplish bags under his eyes had filled out like water pouches. He stopped himself from asking what he wanted, as he knew that Vital would get to the point rapidly. And he did.

"How are you feeling? You look a bit under the weather."

"It's been rough these past months, but I'm starting to come out of it."

"Yes, but now that Charlotte's gone, who's going to look after Trubenne?"

"I will, just as I was doing before the accident."

"But now that you're alone, isn't that a lot on your plate?"

"But I'm not alone, I have Alex to help me."

"But that's just it, what if Alex decides to return to America or go back to her career? You can't expect her to spend all her time in the middle of no place."

"What's your point, Vital?"

"Well, we think you need some professional help to run Trubenne, and I thought that I could help; I'm a business lawyer, after all."

"We?"

"Well, yes, the family. We'd like to be involved in helping develop Trubenne; after all, it's been in our family for ages."

Richard had been leaning over the table, one hand under his chin. Now he straightened up, and Vital felt the chill of an icy blue stare: "And I suppose you would expect to be compensated for your, um help?"

"Oh no, I wouldn't expect any payment, if that's what you mean. Just a share in the ownership."

"I see you've been giving this some thought, so tell me more."

The kitchen chair was a bit too small for Vital's *derrière* and he shifted uncomfortably. He was perspiring, and his heavy glasses had started to slip down his nose.

"Well, you know, there is Charlotte's share...."

"But that belongs to Alex and me now."

"Yes, but I, that is, we were thinking that perhaps Alex might not want the, um, responsibility of running Trubenne, and I could help her in exchange for part of her share."

"Have you spoken to Alex about your idea?"

"Not yet, actually, I thought that maybe you could...."

"I see."

Richard remembered one hot summer day in Trubenne. He had been sitting on the lawn, watching a cat play with a salamander it had captured. He looked at the fat salamander sitting across from him: "Is that all? I sense that you've got something else on your mind, am I mistaken?"

Vital should have known better, should have heard the aggressive tone in Richard's voice, felt the heat of the piercing steely blue gaze. But he had taken "I see" for acquiescence, and so he continued down the dead-end street:

"Well, we were thinking that maybe, and I do mean maybe, you might be finding this apartment a bit too large, now that Chloe has been gone all these years and that, you know, maybe you'd be more comfortable someplace a bit smaller. With some full-time personnel."

"I see."

"Well, it was just a thought, you know. It's only that we are concerned about you."

"Yes, I can see that."

"Well...."

Richard stood up, his chair made a scraping sound: "Vital, if you say 'well' one more time, I may not be able to stop myself from slapping you. Let me see you out," and he gently put his arm on Vincent's ample back and guided him to the entry hall.

"Please thank the family for their interest, but neither Alex nor I will be transferring any shares to you. And I am not moving into a fancy retirement home to die. I trust I've put your mind at ease?"

Richard had always loved a good fight. The morning spent with Vital had given him new energy, pulled him out of his lethargy following Charlotte's death. He called his *Notaire*; he would make doubly sure that all his affairs were in order. He made his plans to go to Trubenne. The image of Vital as a salamander had awaked memories of his happy boyhood summers spent at the old château. He looked forward to returning and closing the circle.

#   #   #

Alex and Eugene left Vauban—weighed down by too many memories of Charlotte— and moved to the neighborhood of Malmousque. The house there was small, but it had a terrace overlooking the sea, where they were sitting. She rested her head on his shoulder, "What are you going to do now that you found the files the Bureau was after?"

"I'd like to help you and Richard develop Trubenne." He brushed aside a stray strand of hair and kissed her forehead. "That is if you'll have me."

"What kind of a question is that? Of course."

"And there's something else: I still want to find Jacques if he's alive. I suspect he knew Aunt Madeleine's brother Viktor." If she had learned one thing, it was not to ask questions. If Eugene wanted to confide in her, he would.

"I've meant to tell you more about my family, but something or someone always pops up. This seems to be the right moment, there's nothing but the sea and the gulls. When my sister was born, my mother had a difficult delivery, and it turned out that she couldn't have any more children. My parents were disappointed—they had wanted a bunch of kids. Enter Aunt Madeleine. The one who left the fake Poussin to my sister. I think I already told you that she was not really my aunt, just a close friend of the family. Anyhow, Madeleine said there were so many orphans in Ukraine, she was sure she could find the right baby for them. My parents put in their order for a boy, blond and blue-eyed. Instead, they got me," he chuckled.

"When my parents told me I had been adopted, I asked them who my birth parents were. I was going to say my 'real parents,' but for me, Steven and Edith Spector were my real parents. They couldn't answer me: Madeleine had said she'd located me through friends of friends and didn't know who the birth parents were. And did it really matter? Of course, it mattered to me, but I had to accept that I would never know." Alex sat very still; she felt that if she moved, Eugene would stop talking.

"Yet, it bothered me that my parents—the biological ones—never tried to know anything about me. Was I happy, where was I living, did I do well in school, play sports, you know, that kind of thing. It was a thought that stayed hidden in the corners of my mind, popping out at random moments to remind me of what was missing. When I was at my sister's place for Thanksgiving last year I was going through my belongings in her basement, and I happened to come across a box with Madeleine's correspondence. They were mostly letters from her friends, but there were two letters from her brother Viktor. In one, he asks about "the boy," how is he doing. And in the other, he tells her that he's found a solution to a problem. A short time after he wrote that last letter, she learned that he had died.

"Do you think you're the boy Viktor referred to? Do you think he was your father?"

"That's what I'm trying to find out. I checked the Bureau's archives, and I discovered a Viktor Karnoski, who was a commodities trader, and another Viktor Konarski, who was a museum director."

"So, you think they are one and the same person?"

"I don't know. But one document I consulted mentioned that Karnoski, the trader had dealings with a Frenchman who was working in Russia at the time. Later, I found out that Jacques Mornnais was there at that time, getting in on the rape of the Russian economy."

"Yes, but what does that have to do with the museum director? I'll bet there are hundreds of Viktor Konarskis in Ukraine."

"True, but Madeleine's maiden name was Konarski, so I'm guessing that the museum director might have been her brother."

"I'm not following you, Eugene. What does Jacques Mornnais have to do with the museum director?"

"Do you remember the files that I brought back from the château? I turned all of them over to the embassy, except for the one marked 'Ukraine.' In it, there was a single folder with a list of paintings, and I'm wondering if Jacques didn't get them from the museum. If he did, then he knew the museum director, who might be Madeleine's brother."

"It all sounds pretty 'iffy' to me. Anyhow, Jacques has disappeared, hasn't he? Or maybe he's dead. And even if you did find him, why should he talk to you? After all, you stole his records, didn't you?"

"Yes, but he doesn't know that, does he? He's a despicable man, but I need to talk to him, see if he knew Madeleine's brother Viktor. The problem is that right now, all I can do is hope that he'll turn up one of these days.

Alex looked into Eugene's eyes—the gold flecks shone in the early spring sunlight—and turned to gaze the sapphire blue sea. Tears spilled out of her eyes, running down her cheeks, dripping off her chin. Charlotte. An image of the fatal afternoon arose, as it would do when she least expected it. A moment before, she was happily talking with Eugene. And now, once again, she relived the horror of the shooting. Eugene put his arm around her, drawing her closer to him.

"The unfairness of it all, it makes me so angry. I keep thinking 'what-if': what if it had been too windy to go sailing, what-if I didn't ask Sauveur to stop so that I could take some photos? Why was it Charlotte's fate to be shot?"

"Alex, you need to stop tormenting yourself. There's no answer to your question, except that fate doesn't take sides. Let it go, Alex. Let it go."

The hot sun had dried her tears, and for the time being, the sadness lifted.

"I meant to tell you: I found a message from my cousin Vital—he was at the dinner Richard had last Christmas. I think he said he was a lawyer, he reminded me of an ugly fat bug. Anyhow, he asked me to call him, I wonder what he wanted."

She turned her attention to a seagull that had landed on the street below to pick its way through an open plastic bag full of refuse. Its foray completed, the bird was airborne, circling out over the water.

"It's disgusting the way people drop their garbage like that. I'm going to go down and throw it away properly."

"You do that. And don't worry about your cousin Vital, let me know if he calls you again."

\#   \#   \#

In the depths of the night, a dark blue van drove through the town of Vélizy-Villacoublay—it had no flashing lights or sirens—and cut a silent passage to the Villacoublay Military Airport.

Once inside the airport, the van drove to a hangar; the hangar's doors were open, so the vehicle was expected. The driver and the passenger sitting next to him alighted. Together, they opened the van's rear doors and slid a stretcher down the ramp that they had lowered, taking care not to disturb the IV pole next to the gurney.

The two men barely glanced at the body strapped to the stretcher. A doctor bent over the body, checked the vital signs, and, satisfied that all was in order, directed the two men to load the package into the airplane parked further back in the hangar. A tall man, who'd been sitting in the van's passenger seat, boarded the airplane, taking his place behind the pilots.

A short time later, the plane took off, heading east. Several hours later, it landed in a military airport in a small country with a somewhat checkered history. A different doctor boarded the aircraft and removed the IV drip. The patient was now awake, and he was transferred to a wheelchair before being disembarked. He was alert and started to speak. With a dismissive gesture, the tall man snapped, "Not now."

The doctor had been accompanied by a young man in a blue-gray fleece, and they joined the tall man in a van—this time, it was black—as the wheelchair was lifted into the van's rear. It was still dark as the van pulled out of the airport, but the sun had fully risen by the time they reached their destination.

The three men ate breakfast together, and the patient was served his meal in an adjoining room. Afterward, the doctor examined him carefully and suggested that he might wish to shower before meeting with his two companions. The patient now realized where he was; he asked no questions but went to the bathroom, where he enjoyed a long, hot shower. He changed into fresh clothing in the bedroom and went downstairs, where the two men were waiting for him.

"What is the meaning of this? What the fuck is going on?" the patient snapped as he walked into the salon.

The tall man sighed as though dealing with a troublesome child. "You went way over the line, Jacques. Way over. People were upset, and we agreed I'd have a word with you, which is what we're doing."

"This is an outrage. All I need to do is call Jean-Daniel Blanquer. He'll set you straight and put an end to this charade."

"Actually, it's Jean-Daniel who tasked us with having a word with you, so why don't you sit down and listen."

Jacques Mornnais turned pale, felt weak in the knees, and lowered himself into a fauteuil. He tried to show that he was unafraid; "Okay, what is it that you want?"

But the tall man was not to be put off and continued as though Jacques hadn't spoken. He placed two BlackBerrys on a coffee table. "Here are your phones. You will continue to manage the Brezikstan relationship, but you're to stay squarely between the white lines, get it? If you deviate ever so slightly, all deals are off. I hope I'm being clear. Pierre here"—he pointed to the young man in the blue-gray fleece—"he's your contact at the embassy. If you have a question, you can call him. You're not to bother anyone in Paris. Even if you try, they won't take your call." He let the meaning sink in; the power equation had changed; Jacques' protected status had sunk to the bottom of his swimming pool.

Kenneth Petit stood up. He'd always disliked Jacques Mornnais, and humiliating the man gave him no small pleasure. However, for now, they still needed Jacques, and it would be necessary to watch him closely to see that he followed the rules. But also to protect him from those who might wish him harm.

\#   \#   \#

Bruno now looked forward to his dreams. When he got into bed, he wondered what small gap in his memory would be filled-in as he slept. That night he dreams of clean, narrow cobblestone streets, bordered by rose-colored brick buildings. There are no faces in the windows, just blank white spaces; the windows are shuttered from the inside. A building looms in the distance, he sees a round roof and a tower, they dissolve into nothingness as he approaches. He feels very hot, and then a biting cold wind chills him to the bone. He sniffs the air, but he cannot smell the sea.

The dream stayed with him as he traveled to Lyon; it tickled his mind as he made his way to Chez Michel. He sat at a purple metal table in front of the café, drank an espresso, and ordered a second one as he read through Sandra's mail. There was nothing of importance, and he threw the pile of paper into a refuse bin and went back inside to see Michel.

"*Alors,* Bruno, we're back in Lyon, are we?"

"Just passing through. Thanks for taking care of Sandra's mail."

The big man wore an air of mystery like a second skin. He'd never been violent, had never even raised his voice, yet he was disquieting. Although Michel was curious, he dared not ask Bruno about his plans.

Michel came out from behind the bar, carrying a spray bottle and a rag and started to polish a mirror that hung on the wall. It was an old, Italian-style mirror that he'd found at a street market. It had an intricate lacy gold leaf frame, and Michel thought it gave a bit of cachet to the café. He felt Bruno's gaze on his back.

"I see that you like my mirror — it's beautiful, isn't it?"

Bruno gave no sign that he'd heard Michel. He'd seen a mirror like that once before. They had been on a class trip to visit Saint Stephen's cathedral, the mirror hung in the entry of the house where they had spent the night. He saw the cathedral clearly now, the low round roof, the tower, and the different buildings that made up the whole edifice. He answered Michel's unasked question: "I'm going to Toulouse, I'll be back in a month to check on the mail."

THE END

Want to learn more about the world and characters
of FRENCH DECEPTION?

Go to janicenagourney.com for the backstories.

CASTLE BRIDGE MEDIA RECOMMENDS...

If you liked this book, you might also enjoy reading the following titles from Castle Bridge Media available on Amazon or by order at your favorite book store:

Animal Charmer
By Rain Nox

Austinites
By In Churl Yo

Bloodsucker City
By Jim Towns

The Burning Gem
By Don Sawyer

THE CASTLE OF HORROR
ANTHOLOGY SERIES
Volume 1
Volume 2: *Holiday Horrors*
Volume 3: *Scary Summer*
Stories
Volume 4: *Women Running*
From Houses
Volume 5: *Thinly Veiled:*
The 70s
Volume 6: *Femme Fatales**
Volume 7: *Love Gone Wrong*
Volume 8: *Thinly Veiled:*
The 80s
Volume 9: *Young Adult*
Volume 10: *Thinly Veiled:*
Saturday Mournings
Volume 11: *Revenge*
Edited By Jason Henderson
and In Churl Yo
*Edited By P.J. Hoover

Castle of Horror Podcast
Book of Great Horror:
Our Favorites, Top Tens
and Bizarre Pleasures
Edited By Jason Henderson

Cherry Dark
By R.L. Wilburn

Dream State
By Martin Ott

Dominic
By Lee Guzman

FRENCH DECEPTION
A Forgery in Paris
By Janice Nagourney
A Forgery in Lyon
By Janice Nagourney
A Forgery in Marseille
By Janice Nagourney

FuturePast Sci-Fi Anthology
Edited by In Churl Yo

GLAZIER'S GAP
Ghosts of the Forbidden
By Leanna Renee Hieber

Hellfall
By Jay Gould

Isonation
By In Churl Yo

JAYU CITY CHRONICLES
The Hermes Protocol
By Chris M. Arnone
Necropolis Alpha
By Chris M. Arnone

Junk Film: Why Bad
Movies Matter
By Katharine Coldiron

MID-LIFE CRISIS THRILLERS
18 Miles From Town
By Jason Henderson
Lost Angel
By Sam Knight
Ties That Kill
By Deven Greene

Nightwalkers:
Gothic Horror Movies
By Bruce Lanier Wright

THE PATH
The Blue-Spangled Blue
By David Bowles
The Deepest Green
By David Bowles

St. Damned
By Ty Drago

SURF MYSTIC
Night of the Book Man
By Peyton Douglas
Dark of the Curl
By Peyton Douglas

The 23rd Hero
By Rebecca Anne Nguyen

Vinyl Wonderland
By Mark Rigney

Yesterday's Tomorrows:
The Golden Age of
Science Fiction Movies
By Bruce Lanier Wright

Please remember to leave us your reviews on Amazon and Goodreads!

THANK YOU FOR SUPPORTING INDEPENDENT PUBLISHERS AND AUTHORS!

castlebridgemedia.com